ASK *the* SUN

He Dong

Translated from the Norwegian by
Katherine Hanson

WOMEN IN TRANSLATION
Seattle

Originally translated from Chinese to Norwegian by Hu Ying and Thor Sørheim with the assistance of He Dong. Original Norwegian title: *Spør solen.* Published by arrangement with Gyldendal Norsk Forlag. Copyright © Gyldendal Norsk Forlag 1995.

English Translation Copyright © 1997 by Katherine Hanson

Publication of this book was made possible in part with financial support from the National Endowment for the Arts and Norwegian Literature Abroad.

Cover design by Clare Conrad
Text design by Rebecca Engrav

Library of Congress Cataloging-in-Publication Data
He, Dong, 1960–
    [Spør solen. English]
    Ask the sun / He Dong : translated from Norwegian by Katherine Hanson.
        p.   cm.
    ISBN 1-879679-10-8 (alk. paper)
    1. China—History—Cultural Revolution, 1966–1969—Fiction. 2. Short stories, Norwegian—Translations into English. I. Hanson, Katherine, 1946– .
II. Title.
PT8951.18.E15S6613   1997
839.8'2374—dc21   97-18111
                                                                                            CIP

First Edition, October, 1997
Printed in the United States

Women in Translation
523 North 84th Street
Seattle, Washington 98103

Not so very long ago
the Middle Kingdom had a sun
whose name was Mao Zedong.
He called China's children
morning suns. Today
I ask the sun.

For my eagle

CONTENTS

NINE 3

SALTWATER CREEK 17

JUST A GAME 37

ALWAYS CLOUDY 57

WE LOVE CHAIRMAN MAO 75

LITTLE BALL 91

Glossary 99

ASK THE SUN

NINE

Time, which always flows relentlessly onward, has carried me into a new phase. I am living a quiet and peaceful life, but this phase is also marked by something else: The memory of an enemy.

Even in this quiet and peaceful existence, I have been under the spell of this memory for a long time, how long I don't know. I've tried to determine what color the memory is, but I haven't succeeded. It feels like I'm caught in an elusive net. I see the face of a close friend. But I also see the eyes of a sworn enemy. Two identical expressions, but one is full of hostility. Calmly I count to myself: three, four, six and a half. This net, with the colorful pattern of my friends on the one side, and on the reverse side, in the shadow, a tangled web of the arms and legs of my enemies. This net, with its splendid images, at the same time contained something that tore my soul to shreds.

Maybe I was sick. Never before had I heard the ticking of the clock so clearly. Every tick brought to mind high, foaming waves beating against the horizon.

"Aunt Huang is dead," Mother wrote at the end of a letter I got yesterday. Like a little postscript.

Aunt Huang, my childhood enemy. The net turned inside out once again. There in my chaotic consciousness was Aunt Huang, holding her hands out toward me.

We followed each other in silence to a distant past. . . .

When I was seven years old, the Great Proletarian Cultural Revolution started, sweeping across the entire country, my peaceful and harmonious home as well. First Father was banished to an unknown location. Later Mother and my brother were also sent out to the countryside. Only Grandmother and I were left behind. One age seven and one seventy-three. We helped each other survive.

Children without parents are like a kite without string. I remember I was outdoors playing hide-and-seek all day long. But as much as I liked being outdoors, I never forgot to go home in the evening to help Grandmother study Mao's Little Red Book. The neighborhood committee had organized a group study session for members of families with so-called bad elements. In the morning they met for the "Daily Reading." They read Mao's speeches, and newspapers, and they made self-criticism. It was not unusual for the leaders to give pop quizzes to check whether the members knew Mao's Little Red Book by heart. Aunt Huang, a housewife in her fifties, was the chairwoman of the neighborhood committee. It was said that she came from a poor peasant family that had lived in the district where the Communists had first gained a foothold. Her hair was cut short and fastened by two black hairpins. She didn't wear it knotted at the nape of her neck, as was the custom for older women. She walked erectly and had a strong back, and she always wore green Army sneakers. She moved as swiftly and energetically as a stiff breeze. No one knew how much she had suffered before the Communists came. But everyone knew that she hated the old society, and that her treatment of counterrevolutionaries was extremely brutal.

Grandmother was terribly afraid of Aunt Huang. I had heard that two old people from the same study group had been labelled counterrevolutionaries by Aunt Huang. As punishment they were forced to stand in the marketplace wearing tall, white paper hats, there to receive the jeers and scorn of the people. Grandmother feared that she might be sentenced to the same punishment, and therefore read through Mao's Little Red Book a couple of times every evening. There were over ten thousand characters that she had to know by heart. I had mastered all of this at school, and so I sat on the bed next to Grandmother and listened while she read. If she said something wrong, I corrected her. Grandma read very softly, because she was afraid the neighbor might hear her read something wrong.

My friends and I had learned a couple of tricks which I taught Grandmother. If you memorized how many characters there were on each page, it was easier to remember the content. Grandmother had been checked several times in the study group, but had managed each time without any problems. She told me that Aunt Huang had been very strict lately, because she believed there were new counter-revolutionary elements in the group.

Winter in Beijing was very cold that year. Outside our window I could see naked branches that were moaning in the wind. I felt sad. I missed my parents and the time when I played with my brother. Grandmother understood how I felt. One evening she said that she knew how the trees could get new leaves. "Can trees get new leaves in the middle of winter?" I asked. That they could. Leaves made of ice, that is. The idea caught my fancy, and I got a couple of friends to help me. Grandmother explained how we should go about it. First we filled small iron forms with water into which we added different color dyes. Then we stuck a thread in each form and waited for the water to freeze. A few hours later we carefully knocked the "ice leaves" out of the forms. Finally we decorated them with paper cutouts. There were lots of different shapes, like "Little Bear runs down the hill," "White Rabbits harvest cabbage," and "Our red hearts always yearn for the sun." Then we hung the ice leaves carefully and neatly on the branches. A poplar twinkled with colorful leaves in the middle of a cold winter. At that moment the loneliness and helplessness I'd been feeling vanished, even the vague sense of depression that hung over me during those years, disappeared without a trace. To this day I imagine the colorful leaves on a poplar tree are ice leaves I myself hung there long ago.

Grandmother and I went inside. She warmed my cold, red hands against her chest. We lay close together and looked at the fairy-tale leaves outside the window. They sparkled and danced in time with the wind's lullaby, like twinkling stars in the sky. Grandmother told me that the leaves were cold on the surface, but on the inside they were red-hot. "How do you know that?" I asked. "Because if their hearts weren't warm, they wouldn't cry when they saw the sun."

Early the next morning the sky was gray, and it started snowing. Our ice leaves had been eaten up by the night's evil wind. Only two little leaves still hung on the tree, like two frightened eyes. "But their hearts are warm," I consoled myself. Grandmother and I left together. I went to school and she went to the study group.

When I came home to lunch, Grandmother was nowhere to be seen. There was no fire in the coal stove as there usually was at this time. I ran to the study group to see if she was still there. I heard someone crying as I ran up the steps to the meeting room. I tiptoed over to the door and peeked through a crack. Wearing a wide, red arm-band, Aunt Huang was sitting right under Mao's portrait. She stared angrily at Grandmother who sat trembling on a bench by the opposite wall. Grandmother looked so little sitting there, pale and gasping for breath. She was trying to read Mao's *Serve the People*.

I stood outside the door. I held my breath and prayed for Grandmother. She was intent and trying hard, and she did quite well until she was midway through. But suddenly she made a mistake. "Wrong again," cried Aunt Huang. "That's the ninth time." Confused, Grandmother tried to explain. "Yes, yes, I made a mistake—it's three, not four." "What?" Aunt Huang grew furious and pounded the table. "You cunning old traitor. How dare you deceive me that way. You must learn Chairman Mao's words by heart and not resort to tricks. You do that in order to oppose our great leader Chairman Mao." Grandmother was so terrified that she fell on her knees and begged for mercy: "I am sinful, I am sinful. But I do not dare work against Chairman Mao. Never. I beg you for mercy."

"Mercy?" Aunt Huang wrinkled her nose. She walked back and forth across the floor a few times, then said emphatically: "At two o'clock this afternoon you will be on public display at the market."

Grandmother was so terrified that she just lay on the floor weeping. I was no longer able to contain myself. I kicked open the door and with all my might threw my school bag at Aunt Huang. The bag hit her right in the face. "You're not allowed to humiliate Grandmother." I walked over to Grandmother and tried to pick her up. She looked at me, terrified, and suddenly she pushed me away, and crawled over to Mao's portrait. "I am sinful. My granddaughter is also sinful. I beg you for mercy." And then she started to hit her forehead against the floor, once, twice, three times. Her forehead soon turned dark blue, and it seemed as if she intended to continue asking for mercy for all eternity.

Aunt Huang glared at me while she rubbed her nose where the bag had hit. Then she took a couple steps toward Mao's portrait and solemnly said: "Our dear Chairman Mao, yet another little counterrevolutionary has arrived. I shall force her to acknowledge her guilt." When she heard this, Grandmother crawled over to me and forced me down on my knees. When I saw her sad eyes begging me to obey, I gave in. Together we knelt, an old lady and a little girl, before Mao's portrait and Aunt Huang's feet.

"You too shall beg Chairman Mao for mercy," Aunt Huang cried mercilessly. Then Grandmother stopped crying. She lifted her head and said: "Poor little girl. She is only a child, and her head is still soft. Please allow me to do it for her." "Fine! Then you shall hit your head against the floor hard nine times."

Nine, this number, as sacred as a totem, this number that had a unique place in ancient Chinese tradition, this number that belonged solely to the Imperial Palace, this number that was comparable to an unconquered mountain top, from this moment the number nine was branded on my heart, branded along with fear, which I couldn't identify, and with sorrow and anger: The sound of Grandmother's forehead thumping heavily against the cold cement floor, and the sight of the dark spot that spread across her forehead. So many colorful memories have disappeared in the course of time, without leaving any mark. But even today, when Aunt Huang again popped into my consciousness and stretched her arms out toward me, I immediately understood that she wanted to call forth this number nine. And it lay peacefully on its stomach with open eyes, like an ancient dream that had never gone away.

I helped Grandmother get up and the two of us staggered toward home. Two little melting ice leaves came into view a long ways away. My tears were streaming like a waterfall. "Why are they crying when there isn't any sun?" I asked Grandmother who was no longer strong enough to answer me. I also asked myself. A drop of blood from Grandmother's forehead fell to the snow. Then I understood that blood too can change color.

When we came home, Grandmother became very ill. As she lay on her bed, dozing, her forehead swelled more and more. I no longer cried. I was through crying. That same evening I went and borrowed a slingshot from a classmate.

The price was my dearest and only possession, a collection of forty-four paper figures I had cut out myself. From that day there were no more paper cutouts and ice leaves. Even though winter was just as cold. From that day I no longer took part in little girls' games, like jump rope or tossing bean bags. I took care of Grandmother at home and practiced shooting with a slingshot.

I was suddenly grown up, overnight. Because I had learned to hate. I hated Aunt Huang. She was the one who was out there every day with an old loudspeaker, spreading propaganda. That was what had sent my father, mother and brother to the countryside. Just Grandmother and I were left at home, abandoned to loneliness and helplessness. Aunt Huang was the one who made us read Mao's Little Red Book every single night, she was the one who didn't dare smile when we decorated the tree with colorful ice leaves. And now she intended to humiliate Grandmother publicly.

I was suddenly grown up, overnight. I started to take responsibility. I was going to protect Grandmother, I was going to protect our home, even if it was already torn apart. Revenge and responsibility, that's a heavy burden for a child who grew up too quickly.

First I made a paper target. On the target I drew a big red number nine. And inside the head of the nine a new number nine, and finally another number nine inside that one. The smallest number nine was the size of a pea. The target was placed on a stand in the corner of the living room, and practice began. Thousands of times I practiced getting the right movement, aiming and shooting at the right moment. When my right arm got too tired, I continued with the left.

Every time the teacher wrote the number nine on the

blackboard, I lost my concentration. If it was minus, plus or times. All I could do was shut one eye and take aim at the number. Bang, a bullet was shot from my heart.

At the time toilet paper was the only paper that didn't have Mao quotations. So finding paper that could be used for bullets was difficult. I had to walk two kilometers, against a harsh wind, to look for paper in the garbage heap by a paper factory. When Mother sent food money, there was sometimes a little extra. Before I bought rock candy with this money. Now I bought paper, steel wire and rubber bands. I made many different types of slingshots. The largest was as big as a machine gun, and the smallest could be secured to one finger. Some of them could fire two or three shots at one time. They were hidden in jacket pockets and arms. And against my chest.

To get the right practice conditions, I would often hang the bull's eye up in the trees. Usually in the evening, when there weren't many people around. In wind and snow I shot ball after ball. I didn't stop until I'd managed to hit the smallest nine with a series of successive shots.

Two months later I was equipped with shooting devices from top to bottom. Ten slingshots of different sizes and with different functions. But the most important thing of all was that I had become a good marksman.

Having spied on Aunt Huang for some time, I discovered that she walked to the milk station at five to five every afternoon. She was responsible for the distribution of milk. She had to walk by two apartment blocks to get to the milk station. Each apartment block had five entrances, and there was a window in every stairway between the second and third floor. These were my trenches.

The day I'd been waiting for finally arrived. I placed shots and slingshots in a row on the floor, and crouched down beneath the half opened window. The cold soon chilled me, but inside I felt warm from fear and excitement, like the ice leaves. Suddenly I saw Aunt Huang down on the road. At a leisurely pace she approached my firing range. It was as if time stood still. I could hear my heart beating, and it seemed like the wall echoed back. I calmed myself down and loaded the slingshots. I held my breath while I carefully lifted the slingshot up to the open window. I aimed, and *po,* the paper ball flew like an arrow out the window and hit Aunt Huang on her red armband. Even though the shot was made of paper, it contained so much sorrow, resentment and expectation that it must have been as heavy as lead.

Her left shoulder flinched, as if she'd received an electric shock, and she lurched toward the right. She examined her armband and then, bewildered, looked around. She spied a paper shot by the side of the road, and then fixed her gaze on the apartment building that stared back with ten windows. She screamed: "Who was it? You little bastard! How dare you, you counterrevolutionary child . . . political plot . . . " She was so angry that she wasn't able to complete sentences. She waved her arms and stamped her feet on the frozen ground. I hid behind the window and covered my mouth with both hands. That couldn't prevent my mouth from opening, silently, as when a flower blossoms.

For three whole years, every time the number nine appeared on the calendar, 9, 19, 29, Aunt Huang felt a little sting on her arm on her way to the milk station. In the heat of summer or the cold of winter, the number nine was a silver chain linking my hate, my bullets and my sense of responsibility to Aunt Huang's fury, desperation and her wish for revenge. It was an invisible, but unusually strong silver chain, that linked the two of us tightly together.

In the beginning Aunt Huang screamed like someone crazed and the words came streaming out of her in a wild fury: "You bastard! You will not die in peace. You're making fun of me, an old revolutionary activist! I'll condemn you to death when I catch you. Shooting at me is like shooting at Chairman Mao. You'll die in hell!" All her exorcisms, long or short, contained something about dying. But after a few months she didn't scream any more. Her shoulder flinched slightly after she'd been hit, but even in the heat of the summer she wore that old coat when she went to the milk station.

Our milk subscription was later stopped, naturally for no reason. Perhaps because she couldn't tolerate seeing me come to fetch milk after I'd shot at her. Her eyes were filled with hate and disappointment, but I just smiled and mimicked something I'd heard in a propaganda film: "EVERYTHING'S ALL RIIIGHT. . . . "

Yet another winter announced its arrival. Grandmother and I were given a smaller ration of coal than what everyone else got. I had to go to the coal station and buy coal powder. I learned to make pieces of coal. The coal powder had to be mixed with water and clay. The mixture was shaped into forms on the floor and later dried in the wind. To begin with I sat on my haunches and shaped the forms. When I got tired, I knelt and continued my work. When I finally saw the dried pieces of coal burning in the oven, I was so exhausted I wasn't able to walk. In the evening Grandmother tried massaging my thighs, her eyes brimming with tears. I didn't take it that hard. The kind of bitterness and fatigue that is much too much for a child to bear had already disappeared from my heart. To tell the truth, I enjoyed the silent punishments we were subjected to. I saw it as a response to my own bullets. I was happy because I had avenged Grandmother.

Finally Aunt Huang, her irritation at the breaking point, went to my school to speak with the principal. She accused me of being the naughtiest child in the neighborhood and demanded that I be expelled from school. Instead I had to copy passages from Mao's Little Red Book for a week.

But in spite of her efforts, Aunt Huang didn't manage to cut the silver chain linking us together. She was still hit by the fateful balls when the date contained the number nine. Between these shots time went on as if nothing had happened.

Grandmother hadn't understood a thing. Only when the milk subscription was stopped and the coal supply ran out, would she grumble softly: "My poor child, you need nourishment and protection." Never again did she talk about ice leaves or paper cutouts, nor when she again was chosen to read Mao's Little Red Book in the study group. During those times everything was unpredictable. I didn't understand why Aunt Huang was less aggressive than she had been. She no longer arranged so many public meetings. Two old ladies took over her job. But Aunt Huang was still responsible for the milk station. She still wore the old coat, but came and went quietly, and suffered in silence when the paper balls hit her. Sometimes her left shoulder showed no reaction whatsoever.

Not long after Mother had returned from the countryside, the number nine appeared on the calendar again. Then

I discovered that all my slingshots were gone. I looked down into the empty drawer with tears in my eyes. "It's not fair," I shouted at Mother. "You have no right to take them." Grandmother had been dead for half a year then.

Ten years later. The shifting and unpredictable political climate has made me a darling of the times. I was allowed to study at the university, I became famous and privileged. Everything that could be had, I had. I had completely forgotten Aunt Huang, and so had society. I remember seeing her from a distance a couple of times, but all I registered was that I'd seen an old woman. "Open your heart, let the world be filled with love," the song went. Perhaps it was because we had suffered more than is healthy that our generation was unrestrained in its worship of the hit tunes' message of light and warmth. The feeling of hate struck me as completely meaningless.

Quite by chance I was looking in Mother's papers one day. It was exam time and I knew she had some scholarly material in the chest of drawers. I pulled out a big heavy drawer where Mother kept trophies, prizes and old treasures. There I discovered a large packet wrapped in pink cloth. Out of curiosity I opened the packet and was dumfounded— there lay all eighteen of my slingshots and paper targets, and all the holes in the targets had been covered over with white paper.

I had always believed it was only my brother who knew my secret.

Aunt Huang, I think we ought to end this story soon. But how? Are you still you, and am I still me? Do we hate and love each other yet? Maybe I was the one who left first. I travelled far, far away, but never out of the story. When it was your turn to depart, you left this world, and you left completely.

For the first time I feel frightened. Because I discovered, Aunt Huang, that you have taken half of the number nine with you.

SALTWATER CREEK

 Summer vacation was just around the corner, and Mother decided to send me away from Beijing because I was being bullied in the neighborhood at home. They called me *gou-zai-zi*. I was nine years old, and Mother sent me to one of my uncles who lived near Tianjin, a large city that was over a hundred kilometers southeast of Beijing. My uncle lived a long ways from the city center. After almost three hours by train, I had to change to a bus and ride for another hour before I finally arrived at a small rural town, Xianshuigu, which means Saltwater Creek.

The town was situated by the mouth of the Hai river. Saltwater often flowed upstream, branching out through the entire town. As the name of the town suggests, the drinking water in this region was salty and often tasted bitter and tart. When you took a drink, the water swirled around in your mouth, and you swallowed reluctantly.

Popsicles were one of the region's specialities. They were made of saltwater to which saccharine and food coloring were added. The popsicles were as hard as rock. If you tried to chew them, you would feel a sweet and bitter taste slowly creep out toward the tip of your tongue. The more you chewed, the stronger this mixture of tastes became.

For generations the people of Xianshuigu had been salted by the water. For generations they had drunk the bitter water. People complained about everything between heaven and earth, but not about the water. They continued to drink it, like they'd always done. When it got too hot during the summer, nothing was as refreshing as a cold shower in the salty, bitter water. But when their skin dried, there was a thin layer of salt across their shoulders and on their backs. Then they would often lightly press a finger to their shoulder, taste it and jokingly declare: "Take a little salt, it builds strong bones."

There were a few thousand people living in Xianshuigu. They lived primarily from agriculture plus a factory that produced a variety of paper articles. My uncle was just under fifty, and he was the bookkeeper for the factory. He was known in the local community as an honest and high-minded man. He was modest and had never wanted to reveal his capabilities to the others in the town. The reason, it was claimed, was that he didn't want to disturb his ancestors in their graves. Everyone respected my uncle because he had an education. His wife, my aunt, who looked a little younger, also worked in the factory.

They had a son, Xinxin, and a daughter, Xixi. Both of them were at least ten years older than I. My uncle's old mother also lived with them and I called her Grand Grandmother. Their home was a typical *san dai ton tang,* "three generations under one roof," and that made the family even more respected. And as if that weren't enough, a niece from the capital had now come. The house was filled with a lively atmosphere and one after the other the neighbors came to visit. The adults entered the house and always said they had come to visit Grandmother. The first thing they asked was: "How are you doing in this heat, old aunt?" all the while staring at me from top to toe. The neighbor children never came into the house. Instead they climbed up onto the windowsill and stuck their heads all the way into the mosquito netting covering the window. The black pupils stared directly at me, and especially at my colorful, checkered blouse and at my shoes that were real leather. Then they smiled, mysteriously, but also good-naturedly, and jumped down from the sill without saying a thing. But that meant we'd said hello to each other.

Gradually I became more familiar with the town. Even a small rural town in China consists of several distinct residential areas. All the houses in our neighborhood were built with dark red brick and on the roofs were gray curved tiles. There was a small garden patch in front of each house, and there you could grow flowers or vegetables, or keep domestic animals if you wished. Off in the distance I could see the huge wheat fields. Under a blue sky, green stalks of wheat danced without a care, right before they would turn color. Narrow canals of water ran between the dancing stalks of wheat. Sometimes you might see a couple of straw hats floating away in a billowing sea of wheat.

During the day only Grand Grandmother and I were at home. The others were at work. Grand Grandmother was the sister-in-law of my mother's mother; her husband was my mother's father's brother. Since her husband was older than my grandfather, I had to add "Grand" to "Grandmother." Mother had impressed this upon me before I left home.

Grand Grandmother was already seventy-seven years old. When she was married, she had, according to tradition, undergone *jiaolian*. She was short, her forehead was large and angular, and she had bound feet that were small and pointed. It was said that she never wore shoes that she hadn't sewn herself. They all had black uppers and white soles. Her small feet swung back and forth as she walked, or more accurately, tripped along. When she went by the neighbor houses the ladies stuck their heads out windows and doors so they could stare at Grand Grandmother's back. "She's certainly well-preserved," they mumbled. "She must have been very pretty when she was young."

"Yes, just look at her waist, and how she glows!"

"But beauty often has a sorry fate, unfortunately," a third commented.

I understood nothing. I was busy studying Grand Grandmother's waist as I ran behind her.

My uncle's house had three large, adjoining rooms. The room in the middle, called the "outer room," was a kind of living room with its own entrance. During the winter this room also functioned as a kitchen. To the right was a so-called "inner room" which belonged to Uncle and Aunt. To the left was another "inner room" where Grand Grandmother and my cousins slept. In the middle of the courtyard, which was a little garden, stood a large white poplar tree. Around the tree a wire cage had been built. This was the home of seven large white geese, sixteen hens and four baby ducks. Early in the morning I went out with Grand Grandmother and fed the birds. If there were eggs, I gathered them. I had never seen a goose egg at home in Beijing except in picture books. The first time I tasted a goose egg that Grand Grandmother had boiled for me, the delicious taste made me absolutely delirious. I just looked at Grand Grandmother, my mouth wide open, and laughed and laughed.

After that, every time we found a goose egg in the cage, I whined, "Grand Grandmother, boil an egg, boil an egg." She squeezed her eyes together to a wrinkled smile, wiped the sweat from my forehead with her hand and said, "You may have one egg for every five you find." As always, her voice was slow and melodious. It swayed like the branches of the poplar tree in a gentle breeze.

Time had always treated Xianshuigu kindly. It moved slowly and indifferently forward. In the little town the water wasn't old yet, the trees were still green, people never ran hither and yon, they never made noise. The sun was still young, and it always hung right above the town, scorching. It was worst around noon when no living creature could escape the exhaustion of the sun's burning, excessive passion. People opened doors and windows, not a single breath of wind was allowed to slip away. People slept, chickens, ducks, cats and dogs slept too. Only the song cicadas way up in the treetops buzzed toward the heavens with the bold courage of despair, "Zi-laa, zi-laa." As if they too were complaining about the heat, "tai-re-la, much-too-hot, tai-re-la."

After her midday nap Grand Grandmother would swing her two little feet to the market to buy me a popsicle. The person who made them changed the color of the ice from day to day. The popsicles were so hard that they could chip a tooth. I took a bite and a shiver went down my back—it really woke me up. Grand Grandmother wafted her large palm leaf fan and smiled at me. I extended the hand with the popsicle and offered her a bite. She shook her head, pointed at her teeth and said, "They're too old."

In the afternoon Grand Grandmother often took a walk and dropped in on the neighbors. Fourth Aunt, for instance, who lived nearby, or Second Aunt Li, who made such good rice crust. Naturally I was always with Grand Grandmother. She and the other old ladies liked to gather in the shade of a big tree where they amused themselves chatting about things I didn't understand, or that I thought were improper and embarrassing. Instead of sitting and being bored, I played with the kids in the neighborhood. We stood on our hands, threw stones at targets or rode donkeys. Sometimes we just sat there and entertained ourselves with strange sounds and expressions in the local dialect.

There were also peaceful afternoons when Grand Grandmother and I stayed home. We looked out the open door and windows. We looked at the unprotected wheat field under the scorching sun. We looked at the big white goose in the shade of the poplar tree. It thrust its long neck energetically forward and chased a smaller goose, around in circles. We looked at the clouds that came and left as if searching for something they had lost. We looked at a snail that slowly crawled up the door frame, tentative. We looked at the glistening wings of the dragonflies, preying intently on little insects. Grand Grandmother sat right next to the door sill in a bamboo chair that was certainly purchased in South China. While I sat on a low wooden stool and leaned against her thigh. She wafted a large palm leaf fan with a steady rhythm, once for herself, once for me, again and again.

As soon as I felt that the fan had stopped, I knew she had fallen asleep. A couple minutes later I noticed that the fan started to move again. "Did I nod off?" Grand Grandmother's words hung in the air. I stared vacantly in front of me and barely nodded my head in keeping with the rhythm of the palm leaf fan.

It was a quiet and peaceful time. I could hear the old clock on the cabinet ticking gently and clearly, second by second. I could feel every single being's innermost movements out there in the heat. I could feel the heat waves roll toward my feet and slowly creep up to my knees and on toward my chest. But before the heat managed to penetrate my body, it was chased out the window by Grand Grandmother's palm leaf fan. It was a pleasurable and beneficent time. From the sky and the field, love was breathing out, from swaying ferns, from fat brown grasshoppers, from the creaking in Grand Grandmother's bamboo chair and from my soul that was full of nothing. Love breathed in and out, in a steady rhythm.

Yet another peaceful afternoon Grandmother and I were sitting in the livingroom door. We leaned toward each other and looked at the sun scorched, unprotected wheat field. Suddenly the palm leaf fan stopped and Grand Grandmother stood up. Hastily she grabbed the double doors and closed them so that there remained only a little crack through which she could peek. From some place or other I could vaguely hear rapid footsteps approaching.

"Grand Grandmother, is the goose egg done?"

"Hush," she put her index finger to her lips and indicated that I shouldn't say anything. Now I could hear that someone who was crying was on their way toward the house.

Grand Grandmother sat down on the bamboo chair again. Right afterwards someone knocked cautiously. I glanced at Grand Grandmother before I ran over and opened the doors. Outside stood two men, an adult a little under forty, and a boy around seventeen or eighteen. Both of them were wearing white, floorlength garments. The grownup came into the living room and the other followed. I was a little frightened and quickly backed away. As soon as they were inside the door, they fell to their knees and kowtowed. The grownup said: "My father has passed away. We have come to bring you home with us to weep."

Grand Grandmother stood up: "Have you made all the arrangements?"

"Yes, everything is ready," the man answered.

Grand Grandmother shook her head and sighed deeply. She bent down and helped the grown man up. "Well, such is human life, and it's been a hard life your father has lived. Ah, yes."

Ah yes, a sigh, like a cry for something distant. Like a sorrow over something inside oneself. In the stillness of the afternoon hour, in the stillness of the room, this sigh reverberated endlessly between me, who stood there stunned, and the two men dressed in white.

Grand Grandmother fixed her hair with her hands. Her fingers trembled slightly. She turned around and took a couple steps toward the old clock. Her legs started to tremble too. She ran her hand over the top of the clock and dusted where there was no dust. At that point she glanced over at me and said to the grown man: "Tell your father that I'm cooking an egg for my grandchild. When it's done, I shall come and weep for him."

"A thousand thanks. We shall tell him that," the two men nodded energetically and went backward out the door.

Ever since they'd come in, the boy had stared at the floor. As he backed up, he lifted his head, and his red swollen eyes glanced quickly at me. Or more accurately, at my colorful checkered blouse. And then he bowed his head again and followed his father out to the sidewalk. Out of curiosity I followed them out. I saw that the two of them went to the neighboring house and knocked on the door of Sixth Grand-father Wang. The door was opened and the two fell to their knees.

Grand Grandmother went into the inner room to change, while I sat in the outer room and chewed on the goose egg. It didn't taste as good when I had to eat it alone. Over on the door frame I didn't see the snail who used to be there every day. "Why hasn't it come yet? Is it afraid of something?" I thought. I became a little frightened myself and cried: "Grand Grandmother."

"Come here," I heard from the other room. I lifted the curtain and saw that she had already put on a long jacket and a pair of trousers made out of black sackcloth. It was easy to see that the fibers were worn, but the outfit was clean and freshly ironed. On those places where the outfit was most worn, she had sewn patches. The stitching looked almost like embroidery. She combed her hair again and put it up in a topknot which she decorated with a little white flower.

"You are so pretty, Grand Grandmother."

"Don't be foolish. One mustn't say things like that to someone who is mourning, do you understand?" Suddenly she looked very serious and pointed at a dark blue jacket lying on the bed. "Put on that jacket."

The jacket was made of the same material as Grand Grandmother's outfit. It belonged to my cousin who was over twelve years older than I. The jacket looked like a dress when I put it on. The sleeves were so long that I looked like I was wearing an outfit from the Peking Opera.

"There now, it just fits," she measured me from top to toe.

I started to fold one of the sleeves up.

"Don't do that." She slapped my hand lightly and unfolded the sleeve.

"You may never fold up the sleeves on mourning clothes. But city children have no understanding of custom," she said and gave a little extra pull on the sleeve. That was the first, but also the only time Grand Grandmother criticized me.

I left the house then, with Grand Grandmother and two long swinging sleeves, as if I'd lost both my arms. We went to weep. Grand Grandmother told me that the dead grandfather didn't have a name. As he had worked as a carpenter all his life, people usually called him Wood Grandfather. He had six children, but only one son. Now the son also had six children, but again only one boy. His life had been as bitter as the water in Xianshuigu. "What?" I thought in surprise. "Does Grand Grandmother also think the water is bitter?"

Several times Grand Grandmother admonished me earnestly to be quiet and obedient. I was not to weep, because I was too young to know how I should do it. If you didn't weep in the right way, you could scare the dead person's soul. Then it was impossible to calm the soul down again, even it it lay buried in the earth. It would come out of the grave at night and dance the devil's dance with a blue light. Sometimes it kept it up all night, and that was very tiring.

"Do these souls go back to the grave during the day to rest?" I asked nervously.

"Many do, but some aren't able to sleep even if they go back to the coffin. Their eyes are wide open, waiting for the dark. Some souls don't go back at all."

"What do they do? Do they dance in the daytime too?"

Grand Grandmother didn't answer.

We turned into the row of houses where Wood Grand–father's family lived. Streamers of white paper were hanging from the trees in front of the house. The trees stood like terra-cotta soldiers in the burning sun. The weeping streamed toward us like waves on the Hai River. Again and again. It streamed into my ears, into my nervous system and way out to my hands which held on tightly to Grand Grandmother. A stone colored dog wandered around with a long white paper streamer. Every third step the dog wagged its tail and the streamer fluttered in the air making a *hua-la-la* sound. This added an unexpected rhythm to an atmosphere heavy with grief. The weeping led us to the house where Wood Grandfather had lived his entire life. Long strips of paper were hanging from the door frame, white against black, and that was very striking but cold and sad.

When we stepped over the threshold, a lady suddenly came out from behind the door. She cried out and almost jumped on top of us. Before I knew what was happening, she put a white ring on my head. It was made of steel wire with white paper wound around it. The ring was much too big for me, and slid down into my eyes. I had to reach my hand out of the sleeve to prop up the ring. I peeked around.

A medium-sized room where people were standing close together with bowed heads. Everyone was weeping. The tears filled eye sockets, soaked women's handkerchiefs and dampened men's sleeves. Occasionally you might see a pair of blinking children's eyes and a white ring sticking out from between the legs of the grownups before they disappeared like frightened snakes.

Because Grand Grandmother was among the oldest, she was invited to take her place in the middle of the first row. Out of fear I grabbed ahold of her arm and forced my way through the crowd. Behind the wreaths was a huge coffin built of *nanmu*. The sunlight reflected off the glistening coffin was dazzling. The next day I found out that Wood Grandfather had stopped taking orders ten years ago. He had only one wish his last ten years, and that was to make a good, comfortable coffin. He took a couple of years to obtain good materials. He designed it himself, prepared the wood, carved the ornaments and put the pieces together. He followed the old tradition of painting it six times six, in other words thirty-six times. Everyone in Xianshuigu knew that this coffin could tolerate heat, drought, insects and a hundred illnesses, that inside the coffin it was warm in the winter and cool in the summer, and that the coffin had a soothing effect on the heart, soul and eyes. A couple months ago Wood Grandfather became seriously ill. Nonetheless he painted the coffin for the last and thirty-sixth time. When he was finally finished, he was so happy that he got drunk, something he never did otherwise. Since then he hadn't managed to stand upright.

Grand Grandmother cleared her throat and moved my hand that was holding up the white ring. She adjusted it for me and made a sign that I should stand up straight and bow my head. Then she folded her hands on her stomach and started to weep. First a moan and then she broke out in a rhythmic weeping. It was all so strange. A moment ago Grand Grandmother was completely normal, and now she suddenly started crying. While she wept, she sang something I didn't understand. It sounded very melodic. There were many people weeping, each with their own pitch and rhythm, but I thought Grand Grandmother's weeping was the finest. At regular intervals she clapped her hands lightly, two times, like she was keeping time. After that a single wave of her little white handkerchief, which for a moment resembled a sorrowful butterfly in flight. At that moment all fear and anxiety melted away from my heart.

I lifted my eyes and looked in front of me. By the coffin were four men, two on each side, facing the crowd of people. They were wearing white garments and on their heads were tall hats. The hats were white too. They looked like chefs' hats I'd seen at fancy restaurants in Beijing. The shoes were also white, but attached to the tips of the shoes were black balls made of yarn. They were round and nice. I knew two of the men. They were the two who had come to our home. Afterwards Grand Grandmother told me that only the immediate family was allowed to stand by the deceased. If the family wasn't large enough, one could hire people who acted like family members. That was what Wood Grandfather's family had done, hired a "son" and a "grandson." Each of the four men wept painstakingly. It seemed like they were leading the chorus.

I peeked over at the grandson of Wood Grandfather as I stuck out a hand to hold onto the ring on my head. Now I could clearly see that he was staring at me with two dull, sorrowful eyes that were extremely red because of the weeping. For a few seconds we stared at each other. And then he bowed his head and looked at his white shoes. The fancy, round balls of yarn on the tips of his shoes shook in time with the sobbing. It reminded me of his kowtow salutation to Grand Grandmother earlier in the afternoon. I felt my heart shaking a little too. Suddenly Grand Grandmother took the hand that was holding my head ring and put it down. The ring slid down into my eyes again, and everything in front of me faded.

After Grand Grandmother had been weeping for half an hour, Wood Grandfather's son came over to her. He took the hand which she extended and said: "You must consider your advanced age now. You have been weeping long enough, and ought to go home and rest."

"I'm doing fine. Your poor father, what a hard life. I, I want to weep a little more for him."

"Yes, it has been a hard life . . . " I heard no more. His voice drowned in the rhythmic weeping.

I began to see a connection now. One seldom saw people crying in Xianshuigu. Nor did the children usually cry when they fell down or were hit. The reason was that they had a common meeting place where they were allowed to cry unrestrained. People complained about everything between heaven and earth, but they never complained about the bitter, salty water. That was because there came a time when everyone sang out his sorrow. But there was something I didn't understand. How were they able to control their tears themselves? Regulating your own weeping must be a sign that you were grown-up. Then you could determine not only the time for weeping, but the rhythm of the weeping. Then weeping became something beautiful and sacred.

The weeping undulated back and forth across the room. I wondered if the man in the coffin would feel contentment when he heard this heartfelt, collective lament? What was he thinking about? Perhaps about the water in Xianshuigu that he had drunk all his life, or about the fine lumber he had been so lucky to get for his own coffin? Was he perhaps lying in there taking leisurely pleasure in the weeping, or was he tensely trying to count how many were present. Who ought to have been here, but still hadn't shown up. Would he be surprised and curious if he saw me? An unknown, little girl—because that's what I'd be for him. A grandfather I'd never met.

The weeping rolled back and forth across the room in a rising and falling rhythm. Suddenly a child screamed, piercingly and tactlessly. Grand Grandmother was right, children couldn't weep, not at all. They lacked the rhythm that gave peace. I silently prayed that the scream wouldn't frighten Wood Grandfather's soul.

The son of the deceased came over to Grand Grandmother again. "You mustn't weep anymore. My father cannot thank you enough for your sympathy. But I am concerned for your health." This time she listened to his appeal and stopped weeping. She exchanged a few words with the man, then took my hand and together we walked out of the room of mourning.

Already on the way home all traces of sorrow disappeared from Grand Grandmother's face. Her little feet were moving briskly along. She talked about the people who had been there, what they'd been wearing, and she commented on the glistening coffin. She said there was only one thing she wasn't happy about. A wreath had been crooked, as if one of the legs was too short. This wreath ought not to have been in the room. I looked at her, astonished. When had she observed all these things? Apart from her red eyes, Grand Grandmother's face radiated sweetness.

When we came home, Grand Grandmother praised me for how I'd behaved. I'd been good, because I hadn't been frightened even though it was the first time I'd experienced anything like this. So she was going to give me four goose eggs. I stood alone in the middle of the room, confused, as if I were still in the room of mourning. The closet against the wall looked like Wood Grandfather's coffin, and the weeping kept reverberating in my ears, wave after wave. On the other side of the door Grand Grandmother started to prepare the goose eggs, while she chatted with the neighbor ladies.

"Have you been to weep?" asked one.

"Ah, yes. It's something we must all go through."

"True enough," several agreed.

"Did you see the coffin?"

"As shiny and glittering as a mirror," Grand Grandmother sighed. "What a pleasure for him. Good compensation for a hard life."

"How true. No wonder he spent so much time on it." I recognized Second Aunt Li's voice.

"Our little girl from Beijing was with me. She didn't cry."

"Oh, really." It sounded like the ladies were surprised.

Someone spoke in a sceptical tone of voice: "I scarcely know a child who wouldn't be frightened. Was she really not afraid?"

"Not at all. She'll be something important, I'm sure.

Perhaps a high-ranking government official," Grand Grand-mother said proudly.

"How can a girl be a government official?"

"That's right. She's only a girl," several chimed in.

"What a pity," Grand Grandmother heaved a heavy sigh.

I didn't understand everything, but this wasn't pleasant to listen to. I am a girl, I thought. But what's so bad about that? Out here in the country, far away from Beijing, no one called me *gou-zai-zi,* or forced me to do self-criticism or break with my father. But here people felt sorry for me because I was a girl. What did you have to be in order to live a happy life?

The eggs were done. Four eggs on a bamboo pole. One boiled, one fried, one grilled and one steamed. Each one had a different color and a distinct taste. I sat down on a little wooden chair facing the fiery red sun that was on its way down. It resembled a golden coin. I thought about Wood Grandfather's shiny coffin, about the grandson's sad, blood-shot eyes and about the two black, bobbing balls of yarn on the boy's shoes. I thought about myself, a girl who didn't understand why it was too bad to be a girl. I thought. . . . My upper body started to sway in time with the laments, and I chewed the eggs in the same rhythm. But the eggs got stuck in my throat. They refused to disappear down into my stomach. I swallowed hard and suddenly I felt dizzy and queasy. I was hot, then cold and I barely managed to cry "Grand Grandmother," before I fainted.

When I awoke, I was lying in bed. There was a wet, white towel on my forehead. My aunt and my cousin were sitting on the side of the bed. "Where is Grand Grandmother," I asked.

My aunt saw that I had awakened and breathed a sigh of relief. She removed the towel and said: "She went out with Uncle to search for the soul."

"Soul? Whose soul?"

"Your soul. It must have been frightened today, and now it's gone astray. Don't be afraid, my girl, the souls of children often lose their way. Soon Grand Grandmother will come home with it. You must just lie here and keep your eyes and mouth shut."

But I wasn't able to shut my eyes. My head was filled with the wildest fantasies. Had I lost my soul? How did it happen? It must be dark out now. Could my soul have turned into a blue light out in the fields? The wild thoughts were interrupted by anxious steps outside.

"Grandmother has returned," Xixi said.

"Grand Grandmother." I bolted from the bed. Frightened, Aunt tried to hold me down. "No, you don't. Do you want your soul back, or not? Lie down again, shut your eyes and be absolutely still. Otherwise your soul will never come back again."

Almost at the same time I heard people coming into the room. They came over to the bed. I lay still as a mouse, eyes closed.

"Is she still sleeping?" It was Uncle who spoke.

"Yes," answered Aunt.

At that point the room became completely quiet. I felt only light puffs of air, as if someone was waving a large fan above my head. I was terribly curious and peeked out from under one eyelid: Grand Grandmother was sitting very close to the bed. Her face was hidden behind a black veil. She was holding a long bamboo pole which she swung back and forth.

On the end of the pole hung the checkered blouse I'd been wearing when I came. Now there were clumps of earth all over it. Grand Grandmother waved the pole, up and down, to the right and left, making the dust swirl. Imagine that an old lady can be so spry!

Gui, Grand Grandmother cried, and lightening quick she flipped the blouse off the pole so that it fell right down onto my face. Shocked and frightened, I jumped out of bed, tore away the blouse and burst out crying. Through my tears I saw that the whole family was gathered around me, eyes staring. They all sighed in relief and smiled lovingly.

"Finally the soul has returned," Aunt said happily.

Grand Grandmother took off the black veil and gave me a friendly look, as always, "I said you were good, but you were frightened nonetheless." She turned around, lay the veil on the back of the chair and mumbled, "Ah, yes. It's something we must all go through."

I didn't get up for dinner. The eggs were still fighting with each other in my stomach. I lay in bed and thought about my soul. What did a soul look like? What color was it? Where had it been this afternoon? Had it been out in the fields? I thought about Wood Grandfather's soul. If it was frightened, it would come out at night, and dance and shine, like lightening on the earth, glittering and unsettled. Grand Grandmother said that it was something everyone must go through. What did she mean by "it?" Were those the lost, frightened and wandering souls of children and grownups, souls of the living and the dead, moving like snow-white clouds up there, against the blue sky? Like colorful dragons up in the blue yonder? Grand Grandmother just shouted *gui* and my soul came back. It was unbelievable.

What a sorceress Grand Grandmother was!

They were finished eating.

Aunt said, "Mother, I'm going with the children to weep for Wood Grandfather."

"Fine."

"Mother, I'll go over too then, and weep a little." That was Uncle's faint voice.

JUST A GAME

"Can my sister play too, please? She can just play defense, you know, nothing else."

"No!" I answered impatiently.

"Let's include her," Bayue pleaded once again. Behind him stood his little sister, Shiyue, clad in Mao-green. She was only six years old, two or three years younger than the rest of us. She looked at us with anxious eyes, her pupils darting here and there.

"She promised me this morning that she wouldn't start crying, no matter what."

"No, she can't play. We've lost three times because of her," I said firmly.

Shiyue drew her shirt-tail up to her mouth and started to chew. This brother and sister were always dressed in green, almost all year round. The clothes were sewn from their father's uniform; the color, in other words, was genuine Mao-green! The rest of us were so jealous that we often grabbed

37

onto their clothes just to feel the fabric. It was during the summer and even in the evening the temperature could be 80 degrees. Their jackets were full of white sweat marks and looked like they were covered with spider webs. The neighbors often asked: "Aren't you too warm, Shiyue?" Then she would shake her head vehemently and hide. It seemed as if she were afraid someone was going to take her jacket away.

Step by step she backed out of the fortress we had drawn on the hill. She sat on her haunches and looked up at Bayue with a foolish smile. We had started playing "storm the fortress" with the kids from the neighboring apartment building quite some time ago. The playground was an open space between two buildings where no grass grew. "Storm the fortress" was a game for which we first drew, with a stick or a stone, two fortresses facing each other. There was a tower at the far end of each fortress, and a corridor leading out to the enemy's fortress. This was the only exit from the fortress. The object of the game was to try and get out of our own fortress, enter the enemy's and touch their tower with one foot. The first team to do so was the winner of that round. Anyone who was shoved or pulled over the line in the course of the battle, was out of the game.

The game was very popular. In the first place, it was simple. All we needed was a playground and some players. In the second place, the game involved fighting, and that was in keeping with the grandiose and aggressive Cultural Revolution. You pushed me and I shoved you. We grabbed each other by the arm and ripped the buttons off each other's jackets. We were soldiers with a firm grip, and in the midst of the chaos someone or other inexplicably managed to get their foot on the enemy tower. The winners jumped for joy while the losers were glum and despondent.

We lived in a university district. The entire University was divided into two opposing factions on ideological grounds. Everyone had to choose sides, students, professors and staff. One of the factions was called "The Soldiers' Army" and the other called itself "Jinggang Shan." Both groups declared themselves to be Mao's loyal troops, and both fought for Maoism. But they accused each other of being counterrevolutionairies and anti-Maoists. They put up wall posters publicizing and criticizing each others' counter-revolutionary actions. They beat on drums and gongs and organized extensive demonstrations against each other. The University had been turned into a lively marketplace.

At exactly six o'clock in the evening music sounded from the huge loudspeaker that hung from a willow tree at one end of the apartment building. The University's radio station began its evening broadcast. There were reports of mass meetings, critical articles and new directives for the class struggle. At that time the grownups were either on their way home from work or, if they were lucky, already home in the kitchen preparing dinner. No matter what they were doing, they listened carefully to what came streaming out from the hanging loudspeaker. The last thing on their minds just then were children. In time with the majestic, revolutionary songs, the loud, emotionally charged slogans and Mao quotations that were broadcast across the area, and in time with the branches of the willow tree that were dancing so beautifully in the breeze of a summer evening, we children played with heightened energy. We fought, screamed and bled. The grownups walking by the playfield never paid any attention to what they saw. Some of them might sigh, "Kids, all they do is cause trouble," and continue on their way.

One day when we were going to play "storm the fortress" with the kids in the neighboring building, Qiang-qiang, one of the kids we played with most often, stood in the middle of their fortress, hands on his hips, and declared that they had formally organized a team whose name was "The Soldiers' Army." That was the name of the faction at the University in which Qiang-qiang's mother played a leading role. Proudly he added, "We are Chairman Mao's red children, and you guys are a bunch of *heibang.*"

"Ha ha, ha ha," laughed the others in unison.

How stupid! We immediately withdrew from the game. I became very sad. To me it felt like I truly was a *heibang* who had been publically shamed. My parents were in the "Jinggang Shan" faction which was considerably larger than "The Soldiers' Army." But Mother and Father were regarded as bad elements by their own comrades and so I didn't dare use "Jinggang Shan" as the name of our team. This bothered me all evening.

The next afternoon it rained, but it cleared up again before the sun disappeared from the horizon. I called Liangliang, Ming-ming, Li Peng, Little Liuzi, Bayue and Shiyue together for a meeting. It was a crystal clear evening. The heat and dust of many days had been rinsed by the rain and sucked down into the earth. In the hollows between the curbstones around the buildings the crickets chirped brightly and cheerfully. The long, thin branches of the willow trees were drooping, as if they had fallen asleep without shaking off the raindrops.

What should we call our team? We started a lively discussion to find a name with a nice ring, and everyone made suggestions. We would be Chairman Mao's red children too. We wanted to defend Chairman Mao with our lives too. I sat on my haunches and thought, while I dug in the ground with a willow branch. Suddenly I shouted, "There are seven of us, right? We'll call ourselves Big Dipper. There are seven stars in the Big Dipper."

"Yes! The Big Dipper is the symbol of the revolution." Bayue jumped up and down enthusiastically, shaking his small fists above his head.

I was so overjoyed and moved by my good idea that I got tears in my eyes. The same thing happened to Bayue. He looked at me with glistening eyes. Everyone looked up at the sky, and among the thousands of stars we searched for the Big Dipper.

"There it is!" Several voices chimed in. There—at the end of our index fingers—we saw seven bright and glittering stars that made up the Big Dipper. They formed a big spoon in the north sky. They hurled fire and light at our eyes. There—at the end of our index fingers—the seven stars symbolized the revolution's spark and hope. We remembered our teachers telling us that the Big Dipper had enlightened many doubting souls in need. We grew silent and for a moment gave ourselves over to a mystical ecstasy, as if we were in the presence of something holy. Driven by a divine power, we formed the constellation, the Big Dipper. I was in front, and little Shiyue stood at the end.

"Up there is the Big Dipper which consists of seven stars, and down here is the Big Dipper team. The Big Dipper in the sky points to the revolution's final victory, and the Big

Dipper team down here is going to win all the rounds in "storm the fortress." All of us were shouting.

Grandfather Wang was sitting on a little chair outside the entrance to the apartment building, relaxing. He clearly didn't understand why we were so happy. "Hey, what kind of nonsense are you up to now? What's all the fuss about seven or eight, or whatever it is. Don't you think it's already warm enough, you little scamps?" Grandfather Wang had turned eighty, but he still held his back straight and his eyesight was good. The only problem was that he was hard of hearing.

"The Big Dipper has seven stars and that's the name of our team. Bayue was named after the eighth month." I speak to him loudly.

"Hmm," Grandfather Wang nods. "That's right. Today is the seventeenth of the eighth month. Autumn must be right around the corner."

"You're all mixed up!" We burst out laughing. "Bayue is named after August 1, commemoration day for the People's Liberation Army."

"I see." This time Grandfather Wang heard correctly, and then he mumbled: "Ahh . . . Strange names and goings on nowadays. In the old days the names had to be chosen from the family book."

We laughed again. Little Liusi said, "Family book? You're an old feudalist! You ought to be publicly criticized." Shiyue made a megaphone out of her hands and shouted, "My name is Shiyue and that means October 1, our Day of Independence." Grandfather Wang wasn't interested in listening to us any longer. He pulled away and took a deep puff from his long pipe.

Even though we called ourselves Big Dipper, it soon became apparent that we had a problem. Shiyue was not only younger than us, she was also undernourished. She was little and weak, her hair was thin and brown. When we attacked, a little shove was enough to knock her over. When we defended our fortress, she started crying as soon as "The Soldiers' Army" rushed towards us. They knew our weak point very well, and always broke through our defense by taking Shiyue first. So we took her off our team. We demanded that we play six against six, instead of seven against seven. But Shiyue was always with us, usually sitting on her haunches outside our fortress. She followed the games, from start to finish, scratching her armpits while she watched. When we won, she laughed foolishly and scratched even faster. Sometimes she jumped up and down and threw her arms in the air, "A long life to Chairman Mao! A long life to Chairman Mao!"

"What in the world does this have to do with you, you ninny?" The kids from "The Soldiers' Army" always looked down on Shiyue. She always retorted, "I'm one of the seven stars in the Big Dipper."

"Oh, so you're the star that's almost invisible?"

"Yes," Shiyue answered. She didn't understand they were making fun of her.

Bayue always chewed her out when we were walking home. "How can you be so stupid? They said you were an invisible star, and you answered yes!"

Shiyue still didn't get the point and replied, "When they don't see me, it means I'm glued to your back, brother. You're in there playing the whole time, aren't you?"

"Humph," Bayue said, exasperated. "I don't want you on my back anymore."

Nevertheless Bayue pleaded for Shiyue everytime we played "storm the fortress." Today was no exception, "Can't we please include her? She ate a huge *humbao* for lunch, and that's given her lots of extra energy." I finally gave in, and Big Dipper turned out with a full team. "The Soldiers' Army" turned out with seven players too. We prepared ourselves for a big fight.

Just as we were ready to start, we suddenly heard someone shout, "Hey, hurry up! Quick! Someone's jumped out of a window." We spotted a boy at the end of the apartment building. He was running and madly waving a green Mao cap.

"Where?" cried Little Liuzi with a shrill voice.

"Building Six." The boy ran on and disappeared from sight.

We abandoned our fortresses and tore off toward Building Six like a swarm of bees, leaving a cloud of dust in our wake.

A group of people had gathered in front of the building. We pushed our way through the crowd and saw a large rush mat on the asphalt. "What a beautiful mat," Bayue said admiringly. And it really was beautiful, red and green with a picture of a phoenix bird with a sweeping tail. Through a little opening under the rush mat I could see blood on the asphalt. But I couldn't see if the blood was fresh, or if the drops of blood were old. Some grownups standing outside the circle spoke together in low voices, and then walked on. New viewers arrived; they stopped, glanced down with dull eyes which suddenly flashed with panic, shook their heads and continued on. A couple of old men stood on the inside of the circle by the mat. It seemed like they'd been standing there for a while. One of them explained, "It's the couple on the fourth floor, the ones from the Geology Department. They jumped out of the window hand in hand, and they're still holding hands." I looked up and knew who it was who had jumped. The man had a crooked neck, and Little Liuzi and I had given him a nickname, "Crookedneck."

"A shoe fell off in midair." Someone else continued, "The shoe belonged to the lady. It landed there." People looked in the direction he pointed, in order to see the shoe, but all they saw was two or three broken bricks.

"Ah, that's strange. I just saw it a minute ago with my own eyes. It was black and quite new, and it was lying with the sole facing up," the man explained, fearing that he wouldn't be believed. I knew that it was a bad sign to die without shoes. Grandmother had told me that if you died without your shoes, you would be a slave worker in the realm of the dead.

"Someone must have put it away," one person said. Others commented, "That poor couple, imagine dying that way."

"Somebody hung themself last week. Two people jumped today. God knows what'll happen tomorrow."

"But why couldn't they bear to go on living? Well, maybe it's better to be dead. At least you have peace of mind then."

I was a little frightened, and I felt that my hands were cold. I tried to console myself that there was nothing to be afraid of. Chairman Mao had said that death was inevitable, whether you died as "heavy as Tai mountain" or as "light as a goose feather."

According to the grownups, suicide meant that you could no longer bear living. That kind of death must be light as a goose feather then. . . .

Ming-ming broke into my thoughts, "It's not good to die from a fall. It hurts. Just think, from the fourth floor!" I cautiously looked up again. The building was gray and indistinct. It was really high. Ming-ming went on, "My father said it would be easier to hang yourself. It doesn't take more than three minutes. Besides, you don't bleed."

"Does it really not hurt to hang yourself?" asked Bayue. Ming-ming shrugged her shoulders and didn't answer.

"So long as you don't bleed, it probably doesn't hurt," I said, not completely understanding why.

Bayue stared at the beautiful phoenix bird on the rush mat, "The phoenix flies upwards towards the heavens, while man flies downwards." No one understood what he was thinking about.

Liang-liang was the bravest of us all. He crouched down and lifted a corner of the rush mat. We followed him and bent down so we could see through the opening. It was so dark in there. It was strange that a rush mat could keep all the light out. All I could see was a large foot. The sock was as blue as the sky. "What are you doing here?" Someone was shouting in back of us, "Get away from here, kids. It's just a corpse." Startled and frightened, we ran and didn't dare look back to see who had shouted at us. None of us went home. We gathered at the playfield again. The fact that two people had jumped out of a window shouldn't disturb our game. That much we all understood. But the problem was that our concentration was gone. We stared into space and played halfheartedly. The attackers were lazy, the defenders sluggish. I couldn't stop thinking about the cloth shoe that vanished. When did the shoe fall off? How could it fall off in midair? And who had taken the shoe? I also wondered how long it took to fall from the fourth floor. What were they thinking about as they were falling through the air? I thought it was too bad that I hadn't seen the hands that held each other in the air and under the rush mat. While they were alive and now that they were dead. When they came to carry them away, who would separate the hands? They say that a handgrip is most rigid if you're clasping something when you die. Then it can be so stiff that you have problems opening the fingers, even with good tools. In that case you'd have to cut the hands . . .

"Victory to 'The Soldiers' Army.' Victory to 'The Soldiers' Army!'" My thoughts were again interrupted. I saw the jubilant players from the other team, and understood that we had just lost that round.

Evening's dark blanket fell over us. The stars rose through the darkness and climbed up the crystal clear sky. The Big Dipper was still shining brightly. All seven stars were there, none were missing. Among the thousands of beautiful stars, I liked the Big Dipper the very best. The reason for that was my own secret. Counting stars through the window at night was a favorite pastime. I always started with the Big Dipper, and presto, I had seven stars. But after a while I usually lost count, and wondered if I'd counted the same star twice. Every time Grandmother discovered what I was doing, she said, "Don't count, don't count. It's impossible to count stars. You can go blind from that!" But that didn't stop me. I often had tears in my eyes from concentration. Then I got scared. I didn't dare close my eyes for fear that I wouldn't be able to see when I opened them again. But today I was mostly thinking about whether there was suicide in the stars' world too. For example, a meteor could suddenly fall from the sky. Maybe it looked like a person who jumped from the fourth floor. If the sun one day could no longer bear living and took its life by falling toward the earth, would the earth be just as dark as it was under the rush mat? Or maybe even lighter than it is today? One thing I knew for sure, the Big Dipper would never fall. It was sacred. But what did they do up there every day? Did they spend their time writing slogans on walls and the other revolutionary activities we and our parents were engaged in? Were the stars also divided into two, three or four opposing factions? Maybe they were busy counting us, just as we did with them. But could they count how many were on the Big Dipper team every time we played "storm the fortress?"

A few days later we'd again made plans to play "storm the fortress" with "The Soldiers' Army" in the afternoon. It was deathly sultry that day, like we were inside a steamer. In that kind of weather people used to say, "The weather gods are gathering rain." I had an uncomfortable feeling, like both my heart and the sweat were wrapped up underneath a huge rush mat. My heart was pounding. We were waiting for Bayue and Shiyue who still hadn't shown up.

"Are we playing, or not? Where are your people?" Someone from "The Soldiers' Army" started getting restless.

"Has the Big Dipper become five stars?" laughing, Qiangqiang tried to taunt us. Some of our players were getting impatient too. "Can't we start with five players?" asked little Liuzi.

Bayue was our best attacker. Even though we were hard put without him, we did our best with vigorous attacks and effective defense. Suddenly Qiang-qiang stopped playing, and looked over at the opposite end of the building, "Something's happening!" When he wasn't paying attention, I saw my chance to run into their fortress and tag the tower with my foot. "We won! We w . . . "

"Hey, something's happened over there!" Qiang-qiang stopped us. We swallowed the words and looked over toward the building. Right then a delivery bike swung in from the main street and came toward us. The bicyclist peddled for all he was worth. On the trailer in back sat another man, way out on the edge. He was wearing a white coat, had to be a doctor. Several people followed behind. The delivery bike stopped right in front of entrance A, and the bicyclist and the doctor jumped off and ran inside. We ran over to the delivery bike.

I pushed my way forward between the grownups, and soon I was standing right next to the delivery bike. As I was wondering what had actually happened, the doctor and bicyclist came out through the entryway. They were carrying a body covered by a white sheet. Bayue's mother came after them. With one hand she held a little flowered handkerchief against her mouth, but it wasn't enough to stifle her piercing crying. With the other hand she led Shiyue, whose face was utterly pale. Wisps of brown hair hung down over her forehead. The people clustered around the doorway craned their necks, watching and listening to what happened.

"Bayue is dead. The boy and his sister were playing at home, pretending to hang themselves, and by mistake the boy really hung himself so that he died." I heard a voice from behind.

"He hung himself on a water pipe under the ceiling," someone else said.

The doctor and the bicyclist lay Bayue on the middle of the trailer, and then they helped Bayue's mother and Shiyue up onto the trailer. The bicyclist started peddling, slowly, and the crowd automatically moved, making an opening for the bicycle. I noticed that Shiyue's eyes were listless. One hand was holding a corner of her jacket, which she was chewing on, and she was scratching her armpit with the other. Just like when she was sitting outside our fortress.

The delivery bike drove away, and slowly I walked toward home. My head bowed and not a thought in it. Three or four neighbors who used the same entrance as we did were standing in the doorway chatting. One of them saw me coming and stepped forward. She squeezed my arm. "Were you playing hanging too?" I just shook my head.

"Such times! Even eight year olds are hanging themselves." Grandfather Wang sighed heavily.

"It's not the same. You ought to think a little deeper and see the difference." Aunt Liu went on to explain: "When it comes down to it, every death has its background in the class struggle." Another woman nodded in agreement: "Hmm . . . That sounds reasonable. It must be his background when Bayue hangs himself at a young age."

"Ahh. Regardless of background it must be hard for the parents to go on living." Grandfather Wang shook his head.

I couldn't agree with what they were saying, and didn't like the notion that Bayue had a "background" at all. "Bayue is a revolutionary. He's a member of our Big Dipper team."

"How old are you? What do you know about this? Go on home now!" Grandfather Wang reprimanded me before he took another deep sigh. "If you hang yourself, you'll be a hanging ghost. With red shoes you become a matchmaker, with black you'll be a beggar. That's how it is, revolution or not."

This was too much for me, everything was jumbled together in my head. I ran up the stairs and into the apartment. Then I locked the door. I didn't want to think about Bayue anymore. I wanted to forget everything. . . .

The night was deep and dark. I lay in bed and couldn't sleep a wink. I could faintly hear the grownups who were still talking about Bayue out in the hallway. I stuck my fingers in my ears and stared at the ceiling. Way up there, alongside the molding, was a water pipe. The pipe disappeared into the wall to the next apartment. The pipe brought warm water to many homes. We lived on the same floor as Bayue's family. It was the same pipe that Bayue had hung himself on. I'd never thought of that before. I tried to imagine Bayue hanging there, absolutely still. I thought, he was smart to think of playing hanging. He played that he couldn't go on, just like the couple under the rush mat. Yesterday we played "storm the fortress" together, but today he died. He's become a hanging ghost, a terrifying creature. It's not easy to understand.

And what about the red shoes? I couldn't imagine Bayue with red shoes. They wouldn't go with his green Mao-jacket. It would look ridiculous, I thought. But deep inside I hoped Bayue's mother had bought a pair of red shoes for him. Otherwise Bayue could risk ending up a beggar, and that would be sad. My thoughts flew on: Aunt Liu said that everything had a background, but that can't be so. I'm the one who knows Bayue best, and I know he loved Chairman Mao.

His father is an officer in the People's Liberation Army, and the party sent him here to lead the re-education campaign for the bad elements. So his family must be very revolutionary. That can't be the background for his death.

Now I understand—Bayue was only playing hanging, playing being dead. It was a game, just like "storm the fortress." This thought had a calming effect. I closed my eyes and grew sleepy. I saw Bayue running toward me, smiling. Around his body he had a silk sheet that was red and green, with a large golden phoenix in the middle. His face was glowing red. He cried out, silently, "I did it. I did it."

It poured down rain for two days. Occasionally ear-splitting claps of thunder rolled across the sky and lightening snapped like a whip. The wind was so strong that the loudspeaker in the willow tree blew down. The wall posters were ripped to shreds by the torrential rain. Red and black ink ran together with the yellow, green and pink papers, as if embracing each other, before the colors ran down into the ditch. The grownups said, "The rain should have come earlier. It's so refreshing!" I didn't agree with that, because as long as it rained, we couldn't play "storm the fortress."

It finally stopped raining. The sky was clearer than before, and we could smell the fresh scent of early autumn. Some new shoots, that were much too late, sprouted on the willow tree. The Big Dipper team gathered on the playfield again, everyone except Bayue and Shiyue. We didn't say much. Everyone looked a little uneasy, as if we'd done something wrong. Five pairs of eyes couldn't help looking at the entrance where Bayue and Shiyue lived.

"What are you waiting for? Bayue is dead," someone from "The Soldiers' Army" said.

"We have to draw the fortress again." I picked up a stick and, bending down, drew the lines very carefully. Little Liuzi and Ming-ming did it again, twice. The lines were as deep and sharp as a wood cut. But Bayue didn't come. Shiyue didn't come either. . . .

Two weeks passed. Some leaves had already started to turn color, and those that couldn't hang on, fell to the ground. Suddenly one day Shiyue appeared, right outside the entrance where we played. We spotted her and ran over to her. We stood around her and asked how she was and why she hadn't been out for such a long time. Shiyue was clearly flattered and smiled as she scratched her armpit. She answered that her mother had forbidden her to play any kind of game, and that she'd snuck out of the apartment.

"Your brother . . . " Liang-liang couldn't stop himself from asking.

"He hung himself," Shiyue said.

"How did he do it? Shiyue, tell us about it."

"We were playing hanging at home. We put a rope across the water pipe and tried from Mama's desk. We tried a few times, but we weren't able to hang from the rope."

"How many times did you try?" Little Liuzi asked.

"Two times each." Shiyue started scratching the other armpit and then she continued in a slow voice, "And then my brother remembered that Papa had told about Uncle Xu. He stood on a chair that he kicked away. So we took a little chair and put it up on the desk. When my brother had fastened the rope, I pulled it away."

"What happened then? Was he hanging?"

"Hmm . . . And then he kicked his legs in the air and waved his arms a little while." Shiyue explained with her hands. "And then I told him that we'd done it. But he didn't answer. So I went over to him and shook his leg. But he didn't move. And then I understood that he was dead." Shiyue looked blankly up at the sky and scratched her armpits.

"How did your brother get down from the rope?" we asked then.

"And then my mother came home and asked Uncle Wang to help her. I wasn't allowed to watch."

"Are we still playing or not?" "The Soldiers' Army" started in on us again. We went back to "storm the fortress," but I refused to let Shiyue play. As usual she sat on her haunches outside the fortress and watched the rest of us. After we'd lost several rounds, we finally scored a victory, and Shiyue screamed in jubilation. The rest of us jumped for joy too, but none of us noticed that Shiyue had left. The days were growing shorter and darkness was sneaking in everywhere. I looked up and discovered that the Big Dipper had already taken its place. But there were only five stars. I blinked hard and looked again. But there were still only five stars.

After that Shiyue never played "storm the fortress" with us again. But every single afternoon she looked at us from the window that was always closed. I heard that her father had nailed it shut. All we could see was Shiyue's face pressed against the windowpane making her nose flat and round. When we won, we could see that she rejoiced with her arms in the air. We couldn't hear her, but the expression on her bright red face told us she was yelling out loud and playing along with us with all her heart.

Around this time the grownups told another story: A student leader gave himself an electric shock and committed suicide. I heard that he had even shaken hands with Chairman Mao. But then he became a reactionary and was subjected to public criticism. He couldn't bear that, so he put both his hands on an exposed high voltage switch. "It only took a few seconds," people commented. It reminded me of Bayue, and waves of cold seemed to stream through my body.

We played "storm the fortress" all summer long. We won the grand finals. We were so proud of ourselves that we walked around with swelled chests. We told everyone that Big Dipper was a revolutionary team and that "The Soldiers' Army" was just a bunch of *heibang*. We had conquered the black bandits and defended the Party and Chairman Mao's revolutionary path. People heard what we said and shook their heads. "Nothing but chaos." Why did the grownups say this all the time? How stupid, I thought. What do they mean by chaos? If anything is chaos, it must be what the grownups themselves bring about. But we're focused. There's no chaos in our revolutionary Big Dipper team.

I wasn't able to calm down the evening we had won the finals. Was it excitement, happiness or desperation? Perhaps a combination. I walked out and looked at the empty fortress. The leaves started to fall. The breeze stroked my face and gently lifted the blue sky even higher. I looked vacantly at the fortress beneath me and thought about Bayue. I thought about the evening we hit upon the name Big Dipper, I thought about Bayue's moistened eyes, clear as stars, I thought about how we hand in hand formed a big dipper, just like the constellation in the sky.

"Bayue, aren't you tired of playing hanging? What's life like in your game? If one day you can't bear it there anymore, will you play dead and come back to us? We won the finals, you see. We're still waiting for you."

I mumbled. Only the leaves rustling in the breeze answered me, but I didn't understand what they said. So many stars, clear and shining as thousands of white eyes peeking through the holes on a large curtain, all struggling for attention. The Big Dipper was the clearest and most beautiful of them all. With all my heart I told of our victory, but I got no answer. I felt lost.

I stared at the Big Dipper and tried to see clearly, once and for all, if there were seven, six or five stars. But I wasn't able to count. The Big Dipper slowly stretched its graceful body, arched its back and formed a big question mark that hung up there, high in the sky. What was it asking me?

ALWAYS CLOUDY

Yet another cloudy day. Overcast, but no rain. No snow. It's hard to say if the curtain of heaven is smooth or gathered. Because it's just gray and mournful. Like a sad face full of longing, but without tears.

A buried feeling stirs in my heart. Tender and supple it slowly reaches toward the heavens. It's as if I'm trying to climb up and take hold of something, in order to complete a kind of circular journey. Make contact with an old memory.

I'm sitting alone, undisturbed, and am about to be gripped by melancholy. My eyes are like the weather. It's overcast, but it doesn't rain or snow. Warily I chew on this moment, and fragments of a cry from long ago rise and fall like waves on the ocean:

"Moo-jiiiang-zi-leiii, qiiang-cai-daooo."

"Sharpen scissors, sharpen knives."

It was this cry, with its peculiar ring, that many years ago rose and fell over the great, shadow-ridden country. Through the narrow, crisscross streets, and between the densely built, overcrowded apartment buildings. It snatched many people out of their torpor. Housewives muttered, "What a gray day. What a day the knife sharpener has chosen." And they went to the kitchen to carefully check whether the knives were dull, or if they had too many rust spots. In the summer people came out in homemade slippers. They had cut away the back strap on an old pair of sandals. In the winter they threw a blue, cotton-quilted jacket over their shoulders. For the most part it was older people who took their time coming down the stairs, out the entryways and over to the knife sharpener with their kitchen knives and scissors. They lay the knives on his bench and exchanged a few words. "Such an overcast day. So oppressive."

"Yes, isn't it? Overcast, but no rain—it wears down your spirits," the knife sharpener answered, shaking his head a little.

"This knife is a little too old, so you mustn't hone it down too much. Just enough so that I can cut vegetables. I don't expect that I'll be able to cut meat with it again."

"Just put it here, and I'll have a look at it."

"Ah, it was my son who ruined the knife. He used it to cut bone. Just so he could get a *guai*. I'm sure he did it in order to ingratiate himself with that shnful girl upstairs. Look at the knife, the blade is completely bent. What do you think, is there still hope for it?"

"Just put it here, and I'll have a look at it." The knife sharpener always gave the same answer.

After they'd heard the knife sharpener's answer and seen the confident expression on his face, people always felt reassured. They left the knives and went back in. Only a few old people remained outside. They gathered in a little circle and chatted peacefully. And then came the sound of metal rubbing against stone. The knife sharpener began to work.

In a time of red-hot revolution, when everything smacking of capitalism and private enterprise was to be torn down, knife sharpening was about the only independent business in existence. Every time a knife sharpener visited the neighborhood, I wished, driven by some vague feeling or other, that I could sit and watch. The knife sharpener who most often came to us had an angular, dark red face. The dark red color of his skin was so intense that it shone through his thick beard. The neighbor boy, Xiaosan, and I dubbed him Redbeard. He was always wearing a worn and ragged jacket. It was impossible to tell what color the jacket material had originally been. All you could see were splotches of dirt and oil. Redbeard always came with a knee-high workbench on his right shoulder. On his left he carried a burlap bag, specially made with two pouches and filled with tools. One of the pouches hung in front on his chest, the other on his back. Around his waist he had a wide, red sash. It was full of large and small holes, as many as there are stars in the heavens. A light, bronze-colored *suona* hung from the sash. Now and then Redbeard had a little boy with him; he was dark and slight and was called Nan. Thd name means "suffering" and the boy had been given the name so he would be protected from life's suffering. Nan was Redbeard's only child. He always walked right behind his father and looked around with eyes full of fear.

I liked Redbeard, not least because his cry had a special

ring and because it consisted of several segments: First a loud blow on the *suona* that sounded like a lament, penetrating if you were close by and frightening from a distance. After that he gave a good shake to a bunch of small iron sheets attached to a piece of rope. *"Hua-la-la, hua-la-la, hua-la-la."* Three times he shook it. Then he stopped, lifted his head toward the blue sky and the big apartment buildings and cried with his resonant voice, *"Mo-jiang-zi-lei, qiang-cai-dao."* Once again he shook the iron sheets three times—*"hua-la-la, hua-la-la, hua-la-la"*—before moving on a little ways. Then another loud blow on the *suona* and the whole cry was repeated.

That was how Redbeard wandered among the apartment buildings and past the walls with the big-character posters. He paid no attention to the colorful posters, the huge headlines, or the quiet and pale professors and other bourgeois intellectuals who carefully read the posters. The knife sharpener cried to a distant heaven. When he figured that people were busy looking for dull scissors and kitchen knives at home in their apartments, and that some had already found them and were on their way out, he chose an open space between the buildings and put down his bench. He unpacked his various tools, slipstones, whetstone, grindstone and other things. He always placed them in a specific order. At that point he asked one of the children who was close by to bring him a little water. All of his movements seemed so natural. I often thought that this man who was a worker with dust and dirt in his hair and on his jacket, even in the creases on the palms of his hands, didn't need to fear anyone. He performed honest work everytime he rubbed the knife back and forth against the stone. It was different with my parents and other bourgeois intellectuals who had pale faces and glasses. They had to be careful and appear humble, even when they were walking by themselves. They didn't produce anything. They lived off of what the proletariat produced with sweat and toil. They lived like parasites, according to the wall posters.

One day, I can't remember which, only that it was overcast, Redbeard came to our neighborhood again. He sat down on the bench right in front of the entrance and started to unpack the tools. As usual I sat nearby and watched. Suddenly Redbeard said, "Hey, little girl, can you go and fetch some water for me?" I went over to him and took the water pail. What an ugly water pail, so many dents and holes. From that day on I was the regular water carrier. I was happy. I felt like I was working, like I was a part of the proletariat. At school I was always encouraged to dissociate myself from my parents. The distance between me and my parents was great. Both had been sent out to the countryside, a hundred miles away, and I hadn't seen them for almost a year. But the teacher said the most important thing was to distance myself from them ideologically and emotionally.

I gradually became familiar with Redbeard's work routine. Cleaning, honing and then grinding, after that wetting and finally drying. One day I plucked up my courage and asked Redbeard, "Will you teach me to sharpen knives?"

"Why do you want to learn that? This isn't anything for people from your class." He answered indifferently and continued his rhythmic movements, back and forth, holding the knife in his hands. It felt like a slap in the face. "Class," that difficult and yet well-known concept that I had learned about at school when I was six years old, popped up again, right in front of me. Once again the class I belonged to was a barrier to the realization of a dream. I knew very well that the problem with my parents was a class problem. They had been sent to the countryside for rehabilitation through hard physical labor and through contact with peasants and other workers, precisely so they could free themselves of their class origins. But what was I supposed to do to free myself? No one had told me that.

I walked home with a bowed head, still in a state of confusion. I walked right into Aunt Song who was standing outside the entryway hanging up the laundry. She shared the apartment with us. She was around thirty and taught English at the University. She was an elegant woman. On a gray day Aunt Song struck me precisely as people usually said she was: Different.

I fetched a little knife. It was a pocketknife and the handle was studded with real jade stones. The knife was my best friend and I had it with me almost all the time. It had been the source of great envy among my classmates. I showed Redbeard the knife and asked if he could sharpen it. He picked the knife up gingerly and studied it carefully. "What a lovely knife! I have never seen its like. Oh, so lovely. Look at these exquisite jade stones, look at this delicate pattern, look at . . . No, no, this is much too fine to be sharpened, don't you see?" Just then I heard a lot of noisy footsteps, and I snatched the knife from Redbeard and hid it inside my jacket. An agitated bunch of Red Guards was running toward us. They were wearing genuine green Mao jackets and carrying gongs, placards and big-character posters. They went past us and charged into the entryway where I lived. I could feel my heart in my throat. I didn't dare look. A few minutes later someone struck a gong and Professor Kong came tottering out of the entryway surrounded by Red Guards, punching and shoving. Grandfather Kong was close to sixty years old. Right after the People's Republic was founded, he returned to China from the University of Michigan. For nearly twenty years he had worked to develop educational systems in China. But now he was forced to wear a large sign on his chest with the inscription: "Capitalism's errand boy." As they passed by us one of the Red Guards suddenly stopped. "Look here! We have here our highly respected proletarian." He pointed at Redbeard and shouted with a voice charged with emotion. His eyes were filled with love and respect.

Redbeard barely lifted his eyes from the knife he was working on, and was obviously both flattered and nervous. He was momentarily bewildered, but then stood up hesitantly. Rubbing his hands on the sash around his waist, he looked at Grandfather Kong who'd been shoved right up to him.

"You must declare yourself guilty before our proletarian," a Red Guard shouted at Grandfather Kong.

"Yes, I declare that I am guilty. I do." Grandfather Kong nodded with bowed head. He didn't dare look Redbeard in the eye.

"Would you please show us your hands, Master?" the Red Guard asked with respect in his voice. Quickly and nervously Redbeard rubbed his hands on the sash twice more, before he extended them. Two large and powerful fists. The skin was coarse and dry with lots of cracks, and the palms of his hands were full of thick, yellow calluses.

"Show us your parasite hands, you errand boy for Capitalism," the Red Guard turned to Grandfather Kong. Trembling,

Grandfather Kong held out his hands. They were small, thin and white.

"Look! We've just had a vivid lesson in class struggle," the Red Guard continued. "What a shocking experience this has been!" Several Red Guards concurred, as if this had been a big revelation to them. "This afternoon we're having a mass meeting and you shall give a self-criticism with your parasite hands as the main theme. Did you hear me?"

"Yes, I'll do that. About my parasite hands," Grandfather Kong answered, his head bowed in shame.

I stood there and looked at his hands. I'd seen them many times. These were the hands that had drawn my name in old Chinese characters. With a flourish of the hand my name had come alive, had become a beautiful painting. "A long, long time ago," Grandfather Kong spoke with a deliberate voice, "our ancestors drew your name like a fish. An old, beautiful fish. The fish swam and swam in the sea." With graceful movements his hands imitated swimming fish. I followed his hands into a fairytale world of blue coral, white sea grass and thousands of small air bubbles around me. And an old saint with a long, white beard waved his hand and painted rows of beautiful characters. I followed his hands into a Chinese world where Grandfather Kong painted mountains, lakes and wading birds. It seemed as if every Chinese character had a thousand-year history, and every single character had many characters within.

But today these hands had become parasite hands. I thought about my father who had also been taken by the Red Guards. Did he have parasite hands too? I shoved my own hands deep down into the pockets of my jacket.

The gong resounded once again. The Red Guards escorted

Grandfather Kong away. The Red Guard bringing up the rear patted my head and smiled. "Bye-bye, little comrade." I gave a start and the hand in my jacket pocket clutched the little jade knife. He smiled sincerely and affectionately, and I envied him his genuine, green Mao jacket. He couldn't have known that I wasn't his comrade, but a *gou-zai-zi*.

Redbeard smiled foolishly and his eyes followed the Red Guards until they disappeared from sight. And then he sat down on the bench again and resumed the rhythmic movement with his hands, back and forth, shoosh shoosh, as if nothing had happened.

"Do you know the old man?" He suddenly lifted his eyes and looked right at me.

"Hmm." I nodded mechanically.

"Is Michigan the place where they grow a lot of rice?"

"No. Michigan is the name of a famous university."

"Strange name, isn't it?"

"Father told me that it's a university in a foreign country," I responded indifferently.

"There are only bastards in foreign countries. Foreign devils, they've killed many Chinese," Redbeard said angrily. The knife whirred against the stone and was smooth and shiny in a matter of minutes. I stared at his large hands.

Another day with overcast skies. I went to the kitchen to fetch water for Redbeard. Aunt Song came up behind me. "Why don't you invite the Master in for a cup of tea?" I turned around and saw that she was wearing a blue, flowered skirt that flared right above the knees. The grownups often talked about how she looked like a lady from a genteel family. She could sing and dance and had been an ardent member of the University's revolutionary theater. But then she was branded bourgeoise because of her upper-class background. I ran out and came back with Redbeard. He hesitated as he stepped into the hallway, quite evidently flattered. "Oh, such a large room . . . oh, such a high ceiling," he mumbled as he looked around. He turned and noticed the book shelves through the half-open door to mother and father's room. "My God, so many books! Do you read them all?" And then he turned around again and noticed Grandmother who was sitting on the edge of the bed. He greeted her with a bow. Grandmother was surprised to see this rugged man, a complete stranger, in the middle of the hallway. Aunt Song leaned against the doorjamb of her room, her legs crossed, and said, "You must have worked hard, Master. Won't you come into my room and sit down? The tea has been ready for a while now." Redbeard rubbed both hands hard against the sash and followed the swaying, flowered skirt into Aunt Song's room.

"What a muscular body you have." Aunt Song's voice was different today.

"I hope that my husband has more muscles too when he comes back from the rehabilitation camp in the country in a few months." Redbeard was completely absorbed in taking large swallows of the tea. The drops of tea hung around his mouth before sliding down across his neck.

"My goodness, look at you. You're so thirsty," Aunt Song burst out laughing. A laughter that came from deep inside. She walked over to the door and said to me, "Go and look after the Master's things, my girl." And then she turned and shut the door right in my face.

It was boring to sit on Redbeard's bench all by myself. I opened and closed the jade knife, again and again. I observed the green color of the jade floating through the damp air. In the green, damp air I could see Nan's wavering eyes. When Redbeard came back and resumed his work, I suddenly asked, without understanding why, "What does Nan's mother do?"

"She died a long time ago."

"Was she sick?"

"Sick? No, she died of hunger. To save Nan's life, she starved herself to death."

Redbeard touched the red sash he had around his waist, and continued, "She followed me for almost ten years, and all she left behind was a red vest. Since she was already gone, I made it into a cummerbund. It shields against the wind and the red color protects against evil." I studied the red sash very carefully and could hardly understand that it had originally been a lady's vest. It was threadbare, but the red color still showed. The *suona* hanging in the sash looked like a mute, wide-open mouth. But if you blew on it, it would pour out its lament: "So hungry, so hungry." I wondered if people from my own class could die of hunger. I tried to get an answer from Grandmother that same evening, but she was preoccupied with something else. She shut doors and windows, knelt and prayed. Then she sat on the bed, crossed her legs, and prayed. She mumbled quickly and quietly with half-closed eyes. It was impossible to comprehend what she said, but every now and then I heard that she repeated, "It's a sin. It's a sin."

After the day Redbeard drank tea with Aunt Song, she often talked about him in the kitchen. She usually said it had been a long time since he'd been there. Every time she mentioned Redbeard, it was a busy evening for Grandmother. She shut doors and windows and mumbled "sin,

sin." But I was glad when Aunt Song mentioned Redbeard, because then it was never more than a couple days before he blew on the *suona*.

One time Grandfather Kong brought two kitchen knives. Redbeard recognized him, the old man with the parasite hands. He politely stood up and smiled at Grandfather as he rubbed his hands against the sash.

"Do you think the knives can be saved, Master?"

"Just put them here, and I'll have a look at them." The same as Redbeard always said.

Grandfather Kong nodded, but he didn't seem to want to leave. He took out a cigarette and offered it to Redbeard. "You must have worked hard, Master."

Redbeard took the cigarette with both hands and felt flattered. "Oh, this . . . how can . . . this . . . " He stared at the cigarette a couple seconds and then put it behind his ear. Grandfather Kong extended his hands, slowly, palms up. "Look, Master, I have calluses too. Cleaning public toilets eight hours a day. You see that it helps, doesn't it?"

A little smile spread across his face.

"Oh no, why do you torment yourself with this?" Redbeard said with a heavy sigh, shaking his head.

"This hasn't been easy, Master. Not at all."

"No. Physical suffering is nothing. It's easy to live with. A pity I couldn't loan you some of my calluses." Redbeard held out his hands and stared intently at his palms. "If I could live in as fine an apartment as you, and if my boy could go to school and live as well as this little girl here," he pointed at me, "I would make whatever sacrifice it took. Even my life." After a long sigh Redbeard spit on the whetstone and started to sharpen Grandfather Kong's knives with powerful motions. Grandfather Kong waved his hand in resignation. "Ah yes, we all struggle in our own way." And then he slowly walked home. I thought: I can't be compared with Nan because I'm *gou-zai-zi* and he's the son of the proletariat. I didn't understand how Redbeard could wish that Nan was like me. Which class was the best? I no longer knew what I thought.

The autumn wind had announced its arrival and yellow leaves were dancing around. Sometimes the leaves mingled with bits of paper torn from the wall posters. I played with the jade knife and tried to sort my thoughts. After a while the rhythm of the knife sharpening got slower and then it stopped all together. It became so quiet and I noticed that Redbeard was staring at my knife.

"A fine knife. A really good knife." He repeated that several times while he admired it. After a moment's silence he asked, "Will you give that knife to me?" No, I thought, I can't. The knife was the only thing I had in the world. It was my best friend. But . . . I hesitated and looked down at the ground.

"We can trade. You can have half of this stone. Is that . . . ?"

Suddenly I got an idea. "I don't want to have your stone. I can give you the knife, but then you have to promise me something."

"What's that?"

"From now on you won't say that we don't belong to the same class."

"Fine," he answered lightly. I held the jade knife out to him with both hands. I was happy, but deep inside I felt reluctance. Redbeard took the knife and gently wiped the jade stone on the little handle with his coarse hand. The light, green color fell down into Redbeard's dirty pocket. He patted the pocket, smiled contentedly, and then stood up and went to have tea with Aunt Song.

Without the jade knife I felt utterly empty, in my hands and in my heart. I thought about my parents who had been gone for over a year. I remembered the day Father was to leave. Father and I among hundreds of people at the sports field. Father put the jade knife he was so fond of in my hand. He said I must be careful with my fingers when I peeled apples. I remembered him standing on an open, jam-packed truck waving at me. I stared back, expressionless, clenching the jade knife with my hand. I saw the waving hand until the truck disappeared from sight. But now? Now I could console myself by saying that Redbeard and I belonged to the same class.

"What's happened to the knife sharpener?" An unfamiliar voice gave me a start.

"He's having tea with Aunt Song," I replied.

"Will you show us the apartment, little comrade?" I now understood there were several grownups in the group, led by a member of the Red Guard. I was so proud of being called comrade that I went with them into the building. As I was about to open the door, the Red Guard took my hand and put his finger to his lips. "Be quiet!" He tiptoed over to Aunt Song's room and put his ear to the closed door. He quickly took a few steps back, and then threw himself against the door with all his might. I was so frightened by this episode that I recoiled. On his fourth attempt the Red Guard succeeded, and the door was thrown wide-open. Much against my will I was shoved into the room, and I was shocked over what I saw. Aunt Song was on her knees in the bed, holding a sheet up to her chest. Panic flashed from her eyes and her face was beet red. The window was open and a cry was heard, "The culprit has fled!" Several strong men jumped out through the window and ran after the "culprit." The Red Guard went over to the bed and ripped the sheet off Aunt Song. "You incorrigible whore! How dare you seduce the proletariat!" Aunt Song was put on display in front of those gathered. She covered her face with both hands and cried violently. Ten pairs of eyes followed Aunt Song's pale and naked body as she threw herself back and forth in the bed.

"He was the one, that vulgar thug forced me. He . . . "

"Shut up!" At the Red Guard's shout, Aunt Song swallowed her words. She just sobbed.

"The bourgeoisie's attack on the proletariat is becoming more and more demented. Now they're even dragging the proletariat to bed. In the light of day. Insane!" another said.

What had Redbeard done? I wanted to ask him. I was suddenly struck by this thought and ran out. But there were only some old neighbors outdoors, standing in a circle talking. They spoke mysteriously and all ears stretched as far as they could toward the middle of the circle. Now and then one of them pointed toward the window of Aunt Song's apartment.

A couple months went by but Redbeard didn't turn up. I missed the piercing sound of the *suona* and the familiar call. I was sitting outside one overcast day, waiting for the knife sharpener to come. But he didn't. Instead a group of dealers in used goods arrived. They came four or five times a year with their delivery bikes. People in the neighborhood lined up eagerly to get rid of things they no longer needed.

Worn-out clothing, empty wine bottles and lots of other stuff. Those who really needed money, might sell their valuables, antiques and the like. The man in charge of these things had a pretty little cabinet with a lock on the trailer behind the bike. I thought this was terribly amusing and was leaning against the trailer. The man had just bought a pearl necklace and came over to the cabinet. He unlocked it and pulled out several drawers, one after the other, as if he were wondering which drawer he should put the necklace in. Then my eye caught sight of something green in one of the drawers. There was my dear jade knife, as green as ever.

"That's my knife! Give it back to me!" I couldn't keep myself from shouting.

"What? What's yours? Stop fooling around, you little ninny!" The man acted impatient and waved me away.

"It's true. It's my knife. I want to buy it back." But nothing helped. My cry was drowned in the sound of loud voices bartering and arguing. The man didn't even bother to look at me.

Winter crept up on us unusually early that year. The next time I met Aunt Song, she had a big stomach. It occurred to me that it had been a long time since I'd seen her hanging up clothes or reading the big-character posters. But people in the neighborhood were still talking about what happened.

"Good for him, a dirty knife sharpener. Who would have thought he would actually sow his seed here among us academics. A toad has tasted the flesh of a swan."

"Pity for her. She could have had anyone. Why a foolish knife sharpener? You shouldn't degrade yourself that way."

"It's all over for her. What a pity."

~

Even now, in a distant world, on an overcast day, I can feel a painful, indescribable emotion rising up inside. I can again hear the powerful call, intermingled with Aunt Song's bell-like laughter, Grandfather Kong's stories, Grandmother's prayers and the Red Guards' gongs. All these sounds, the voice of life, with their overtones and undertones of longing and tears. And now the clouds have become darker and the shadows denser. I gently close my eyes and wait in silence for a blast of the *suona* in the distance.

If, at this moment, heaven were compassionate, I would hear raindrops.

WE LOVE CHAIRMAN MAO

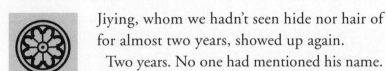Jiying, whom we hadn't seen hide nor hair of for almost two years, showed up again.

Two years. No one had mentioned his name.

He was the nine-year-old son of a Communist martyr and the chief instigator of the sensational counter-revolutionary episode that shocked the entire school. But no one had asked about where Jiying had been banished, or if he were dead or alive. He was like a wisp of smoke that had wafted away to a distant world. He had nothing to do with us. The whole thing was shrouded in mystery, just like the counterrevolutionary incident in which he'd been involved. The school authority and the teachers had devoted a lot of time getting us to understand the implications of Jiying's crime. But on what bright and early morning had we dropped him so completely from our memory? We still went to the same school, followed the waves and streams of the revolution, lived and grew normally, hadn't jumped over a single day.

Jiying's appearance at the door to our classroom, behind the teacher, reminded us that the boy who had been gone so long actually existed. His father was a hero who died in a border conflict with the Soviet Union, defending China's Pearl Island. The son was therefore given the name Jiying, which means "the hero's descendant." Jiying had an exemplary mother as well who printed cards with Mao-quotations. Jiying was always singled out as the best of the Little Red Guards, until he committed his counterrevolutionary crime. He was in his element every time Mao's new quotations were made public. When we went out on the streets to celebrate these occasions, he always wanted to carry the largest banner. He eagerly ran back and forth, and led our class in the parade. He used to fill his pockets with cards of Mao's latest quotations. His mother's print shop had made the cards, and he passed them out to eager classmates.

Jiying followed the teacher into the classroom. A deafening silence suddenly fell over the noisy class. Everyone looked at him, and our eyes grew as large as Chinese lanterns. Teacher Liu stopped in front of Xiaohong, who was sitting next to me. She pointed at a desk in front of us and asked Xiaohong to move. And then Teacher Liu turned and made a sign to Jiying. Jiying sat down on the chair and was as stiff as a board. A cool fragrance streamed toward me. I could feel the entire class holding its breath. And in this breathless classroom the teacher started her lecture, as if nothing had happened. She didn't say a single word about Jiying's return.

During recess I went to the teacher's office and asked to be moved. I wanted to advance and therefore didn't want to sit next to a counterrevolutionary. Teacher Liu smiled sweetly. She always smiled sweetly. She even smiled when, time after time, she crossed my name off the list of candidates for the Little Red Guards.

"You want to be a member of the Little Red Guards, don't you? Now you have a chance to show that." I looked at her smiling face without understanding what she meant. "As far as the boy undergoing re-education is concerned," that was how she referred to Jiying, "you must always be on guard. You are to help him and watch over him. Once a week you will come to me and report on his behavior." She took a gulp of tea from her mug.

One lovely spring day two years ago the entire school gathered in the schoolyard for a mass meeting. Cheerful and colorful spring flowers had been placed on a stage in front of the assembly. Up there stood Jiying's mother exposing and criticizing her son's counterrevolutionary act. Her tearful voice streamed out from the loudspeakers, "Jiying, you have betrayed Chairman Mao. Can you have forgotten how your father died? You'll amount to nothing!" She raised a clenched fist above her head, as if she were about to shout a slogan. But she held the words back, they never came out. The fist, held high above her head, fell heavily down on her chest. "Such a short time, scarcely enough for a couple mouthfuls of rice. Such a short time, scarcely enough for a couple mouthfuls of rice. . . . " The chairman of the School's Revolutionary Committee came over to Jiying's mother and supported her as she collapsed. She was helped down the steps. And on her way down she repeated "scarcely enough for a couple mouthfuls of rice." Jiying was not standing on the stage. Nor was he down among us. He'd been taken away by the police a long time ago. No one knew what had become of him, or how long he would be away. All we saw were the pansies, the "butterfly flowers," on and around the stage swaying in the gentle breeze. Like dreaming butterflies in a deep sleep.

For two whole weeks after the mass meeting we'd conducted a campaign in our class. With big-character posters and criticism meetings where everyone in the class gave speeches. Often the school authority attended the meetings. Teacher Liu, with her sweet smile, helped us to see, from different angles, the counterrevolutionary nature of Jiying's action. What had actually happened was the following: One day Jiying was writing a slogan on the wall of the entryway to the apartment building: "We wish Chairman Mao a long life without limitations." After he had finished writing "without," his mother called him home to lunch. Jiying was starving. He stopped writing and went home. "We wish Chairman Mao a long life without . . . " The neighbors discovered the slogan and interpreted it as counterrevolutionary. Jiying had barely had time to finish eating before the police descended.

Why did he stop precisely at the word "without"? Why could he feel hunger while he was writing a revolutionary slogan? Why did he choose such an obvious place as the wall of the entryway? With the help of the school authority and Teacher Liu we had prepared a list with over one hundred questions like this. After close consideration we clearly saw Jiying's counterrevolutionary character.

Jiying was taller now. The face that was round and flat before, had become long and narrow. His eyes were dark and sad, like those of a seventy year old. His lips curved inwards and his cheeks were sunken. Jiying never said anything in class, and he never talked with anyone afterwards. It had always been the case that when a new boy entered the class, the other boys would immediately demonstrate who was in charge. What they usually did was to form a ring around the new pupil during recess and walk around him. Once a newcomer had been through this, he was part of the group. But Jiying was not confronted with anything like this, and so he was not made part of the group either. They didn't even talk to him. He just sat there, all alone. He bowed his head and sat sharpening his pencils with a small knife during recess. When the teachers stood at the lectern and spoke, he always leaned as far forward as he could and listened with his left ear. It was said that his right ear was damaged from blows he'd received in prison. Many teachers liked to walk back and forth while they spoke, and then Jiying's head kept turning to follow them. When the teachers said something funny, he laughed too, a dry laughter, but loud, and long after the others were done laughing. When the class representative called "stand up" so we could greet the teacher before class, he always bolted from his chair after he'd seen the others stand up. When he then bowed, mechanically and apologetically, the teachers paid no attention to him.

The last class on Wednesday afternoon was set aside for political study; we studied various documents from the Central Committee of the Communist Party. In the recess before class Jiying did not sharpen his pencils. He quietly picked his school bag up from the desk, made his way through the throng of animated and boisterous classmates and left the room with bowed head. He disappeared like a wisp of smoke, just as he had done two years before. Jiying was not permitted to listen to party documents because he was a counterrevolutionary undergoing re-education. Someone who still had to be watched over. And it was my assignment to do that. I had already made three reports to Teacher Liu on Jiying's behavior. One time he'd forgotten to do his homework in Chinese, sometimes he did other things in class when the teachers were speaking, he wasn't very social, etc. Teacher Liu asked me several times if there was anything of a more political character. I was never able to remember anything like that, no matter how hard I tried. Teacher Liu always finished by saying, "Stay on the alert and observe carefully," and then she took a gulp of tea from her mug.

The biggest headache for me was actually not reporting on Jiying, but having to help him study Chairman Mao's teachings two times a week. After school was over, the two of us remained in the big classroom. We sat as stiff as boards. I showed Jiying the paragraphs Teacher Liu had marked with red checks in Chairman Mao's Little Red Book, and he started copying them. The pencil rubbed against the paper with a noise that often caused my thoughts to fly to my friends who were playing outdoors. Sometimes I felt guilty and did self-criticism to chase my thoughts back to Chairman Mao's teachings. From time to time I glanced surreptiously at Jiying. I thought he wrote in a strange manner. His head hung limply forward, almost all the way down on the desk, and he wrote with a pencil stub that was pressed hard against the paper by his large hand. His lips moved in and out in time with the writing. I'd heard that he'd had to perform hard, physical labor every day he was in prison.

"I'm finished," he said loudly and handed me the note-book. As I was checking what he'd written, I usually asked if he had any questions. "No," he answered loud and clear, every time. After I'd gotten the usual answer, I packed my bag as fast as I could and ran out of the classroom and the schoolyard and jumped right into whatever game my girl-friends were playing. How Jiying gathered his things to-gether, which gate he used to leave school, or where he went, I knew nothing about.

And then one day Jiying said there was something he didn't completely understand. "Do you think everyone who's been sen-tenced to prison is a counterrevolutionary?" "Of course." I an-swered indifferently, as I quickly checked what Jiying had copied:

Which standard shall we use to decide whether a youth is revolutionary or not? How shall we be able to pick him out? There can only be one criterion, and that is to see if he is willing to make common cause with the proletariat and peasant masses, and if he truly does that. If he is willing to do that, and truly does it, he is a revolutionary. Otherwise he is either not a revolutionary or a counterrevolutionary. If he today makes common cause with the proletariat and peasant masses, he is today a revolutionary. If he tomorrow stops doing this, or reverts in order to suppress the people, he becomes a non-revolutionary or a counterrevolutionary.

"Among the prisoners there are also workers and peasants. I tried to be with them as much as possible." Jiying spoke quietly.

"Nonsense! How can workers and peasants be imprisoned?"

"It's true." Jiying looked right into my doubting eyes. I thought for a couple seconds and said firmly, "They're not revolutionaries no matter what. Everyone who's in prison is a counterrevolutionary. In any event, it doesn't help you that you spent a lot of time with them."

I was proud of my precise answer and felt a sense of joy. I ran out of the classroom to find Xiaohong and my friends. Xiaohong and Meimei saw me from a distance and waved. They were playing a game of jump rope in which an elastic band was extended between two girls, and a third tried to jump over it. We usually started low, with the elastic band around the ankle, and after each successful jump, the band was moved higher up. I was in top form and jumped as high as right below the chest in one round. Only two more steps and I'd win that round. But Xiaohong and Meimei didn't want to move the band higher up. I asked why not, and they answered that it hurt up there. I didn't understand. Then they started laughing, bashfully and a little secretively, and covered their chests with their hands. "Do you have to ask? Doesn't it feel the same to you?" I became even more confused and irritated. "How can you be so depraved?" I couldn't give in and I wanted to know what was really going on. I went over to Meimei, and without thinking lifted my hands and felt her chest. It was a bit of a shock. I quickly pulled my hand away and felt my own chest. It was as flat as the asphalt under my feet. I looked at Meimei and Xiaohong. Under the bashful expression on their faces, they beamed with pride. A pride I had never before seen on them. A pride that humbled me. Meimei shyly buttoned the top button on her blouse. "My mother says you have to drink milk in the morning so they'll get big." But I didn't have a mother or a father who told me that, or who could buy milk for me. They were far away, working in the countryside, and were among the people undergoing re-education. The money I had barely covered food for me and Grandmother. We simply couldn't afford to buy milk. But without milk would my chest stay flat forever? My heart felt as heavy as a large stone.

We opened Mao's Little Red Book. The day's assignment, which the teacher had marked with a red check, was quite a long piece by our dear chairman. Even today I don't understand much of the text. I smiled wearily at Jiying, but he didn't seem especially concerned. Instead he pulled a wooden T square out of his bag. "I made this for you." I hurriedly looked around to make sure no one else was in the classroom, or standing by the doors. Then I almost grabbed the gift from him and thrust it down into my bag. My heart was pounding. "Is it right to accept gifts from someone undergoing re-education? Is his intention to bribe me?" But I wanted a present and it was much too difficult to refuse to take it.

"Finished!" Jiying's voice broke in on my thoughts.

Gradually my impression of Jiying improved. I started asking myself why he had written a reactionary slogan and become a counterrevolutionary. I had less and less to report about things Jiying said or did having to do with class politics. Instead I tried to put in a good word for him with Teacher Liu. Smiling sweetly she put words in my mouth and helped me refresh my memory. She advised me to keep watch over my own standpoint at all times. "A political stand-point is an important question of principle."

Because of poor hearing Jiying had to borrow my notes so he could get what he missed in class. We also agreed that when the class representative called "stand up," I would rap lightly on the right-hand corner of his desk so that he could avoid embarrassing situations. I noticed that Jiying's rigid face was becoming more relaxed. And then one morning he unexpectedly came into the classroom wearing a genuine green Mao-jacket, freshly washed.

"Hey, deaf man, where did you steal that jacket from?" The boys in the class mocked him.

"It's my father's."

"How can a counterrevolutionary be allowed to wear genuine Mao-green?"

Jiying didn't answer. He bowed his neck and sharpened his pencils like always, but there was something a little different about his demeanor. During recess he gave me back my notebook. A note was hanging out of it and on it was written, "Meet me in the cornfield after school. Jiying." I snatched the note and wrote on the back, "We shall study Mao's works when school is over." He wrote back, "We'll study in the cornfield, that's even more revolutionary."

There was a huge cornfield in back of the schoolyard that belonged to the peoples' commune "The East Is Red." In the autumn the entire school worked there in order to "reap experiences from real life." But during the rest of the year you didn't see many people there. Jiying and I walked on the ridge between cornstalks that were much taller than we were. It was already possible to see little cobs here and there, like tightly wrapped babies. Jiying chattered away, and Mao's Little Red Book was flapping in the air along with his animated hands. He suggested that we play "run after the sun." "What's that?" I asked. He explained, "Every day the sun goes from east to west, you know. If we run toward the west, in that direction, we'll catch the sun. Don't you think so?" Surprised, I looked at the boy in front of me, who was suddenly very different from the Jiying I knew in the classroom. I was reminded of the earlier, energetic Jiying who two years ago had led us on demonstration marches. His idea sounded exciting. When it came to games, I was full of self-confidence. There had never been a game, for boys or girls, that I hadn't been able to play. Such a bold idea as running after the sun had a particularly inspiring effect on me.

We ran through the cornfield, one in front and one in back. We ran toward the west. "Hey sun, wait a minute!" we joked. Jiying ran holding his hands and Mao's Little Red Book above his head. "Sun, you don't have any feet. What makes you run so fast?" The sun didn't answer, it just sped away. Jiying took off his shirt and ran bare-chested. I took off my shoes and ran bare-footed. I can't remember how many times we fell, we just ran and ran, and finally both of us fell and weren't able to get up again. Then I discovered that I'd skinned my feet on the stones, and that his back was full of welts from the cornstalks. It hurt, and we hadn't been able to catch the sun. It must have seen us, and it clearly didn't like being followed. It turned red and tried to withdraw behind a cloud. Jiying lay on his side and played with a little corn cob that had fallen off prematurely. He lifted his burning red face and looked at me. Drops of sweat ran down along my braids. His back was still red from the whip lashes of the cornstalks. It was so quiet around us that we could hear one or two grasshoppers jumping around, and our own breathing.

"Why did you write a counterrevolutionary slogan?" The question simply fell out of my mouth.

"I . . . ?" He was at a loss about what he should say and just shook his head. "No, I didn't mean it, really." He suddenly seemed so deflated.

"How did you become deaf in one ear?" I asked discreetly.

"I was beaten. . . . " His voice was so low I could barely hear it.

"Do you mean the People's Police beats people?"

"They only beat the counterrevolutionaries."

"But are you, are you really a counterrevolutionary deep inside?"

He lifted his head abruptly and stared at me. I, too, was frightened by my own question. A long silence followed. And then Jiying jumped up, grabbed my hand and pressed it against his chest. Outside the sweat had still not dried, and inside his heart was pounding violently. I tried to pull my hand back, but he pressed it even harder against his chest. "I love Chairman Mao with all my heart, all my heart." His shaking voice broke into tears. He bent his head, and his tears fell down onto the back of my hand and his chest.

For the first time in my life I touched someone of the opposite sex. A boy's chest. I could feel the powerful rhythm within, the same as mine. For the first time I received the tears of a boy, warm and clear, the same as my own. I was deeply moved. I no longer doubted Jiying's love for Chairman Mao. He must have loved Mao as deeply as I did. Even today I can't explain what it was that moved me so. All I remember is the burning sun, the endless cornfield and the boy next to me with tears in his eyes. All I remember feeling is that the prologue to the most important act in life had now begun for me.

I cautiously took Jiying's hand and lay it against my chest. For the first time I told someone my own secret: I couldn't afford to drink milk.

It was Wednesday again and time for political studies. I found a new note in my notebook. "I'll wait for you in the cornfield. Jiying." During the recess I saw him take his school bag and leave the classroom alone. A feeling of injustice and compassion came over me. The document read to us in class that day was nr. 207 from the Central Committee of the Communist Party. An eight-point plan to restore order to the rail system. I didn't understand much of it, but it couldn't possibly be anything Jiying ought not to hear, counter-revolutionary or not. After class I found him in the cornfield. He said he wanted to give me a present, and asked me to guess what it was. I guessed three times, and guessed wrong all three times. Jiying smiled slyly and carefully stuck his hand inside his jacket. A bottle of milk. Astonished, I looked at him and at the bottle, and felt extremely happy. My mouth opened wide, but no words came out. "I bought it with money that I saved in prison. I've figured out there's enough money for eight bottles of milk," Jiying said, handing me the bottle. I took it and poured the milk down my throat.

We sat down on the ground. A thought suddenly occurred to me. "Jiying, I have a present for you too." He was excited and reached out with his hands. I said he didn't need his hands, just his ears. Jiying hesitated a minute and then quickly moved to my right-hand side. He shut both eyes and turned his left ear, the undamaged one, toward me. I told him everything I was able to scrape up from my memory about the Communist Party's eight-point plan to restore order to the rail system. I enthusiastically declared that this was my gift to him. "This is the Central Committee's new document that we studied today," I said in a slightly mysterious voice. Jiying jumped to his feet and looked around, intently and nervously, like a spy I'd seen in a film. He bent down and said seriously, "You must not tell this to anyone." And then he took off. I didn't get to see what I'd expected of him, enthusiasm and joy at having heard something he otherwise had no opportunity to hear. I was left in the cornfield, alone.

The next day I was called into Teacher Liu's office. After I'd been interrogated for an hour, I understood that Jiying had reported to her that I'd told him about the contents of the Central Committee's document. I had committed a grave error of a "principle and political nature." Yet again my name was crossed off the list of candidates for the Little Red Guard. I was ordered to stay away from class for a week and make self-criticism. Jiying, on the other hand, was praised for having reported the matter. He was moved to another seat, and Xiaohong was to take over my assignment of watching over him.

On my first day back at school after a week's expulsion, I found a bottle of milk deep in the drawer of my desk. I couldn't resist glancing at Jiying's back, the boy who betrayed and sold me. That day the entire school was going to march in celebration of the publication of a new work by Mao. The school authority required everyone to wear a white shirt and blue trousers. I didn't have blue trousers, so I had to use a pair of my brother's worn-out trousers. A pair I'd found in a closet. The pant legs were much too long, so I had to fold them up and fasten them with paper clips. When we were about to start the march, I noticed Teacher Liu and the Party Secretary of the school arguing about something.

"He's behaved himself quite well lately."

"But this is a matter of principle."

And then the Party Secretary came over to us and motioned that Jiying should step out.

The butterfly flowers on and around the stage in the school yard were as colorful as always. Jiying was led to the stage. He stood by the flowers, all alone, exposed to ridicule in front of all the school children. He was wearing a white blouse. The large, round neckline made his face look even longer and narrower. The pupils started to mumble.

"He's probably taken his sister's blouse."

"Nonsense. His sister died because of him. The blouse must be his mother's."

My heart felt like it was in my throat. My eyes had not left Jiying for a minute. The mass of people at the other end of the school yard began to move, and the march started. I saw Jiying's red back and his warm tears when we were chasing the sun. I thought about how he deceived me. My class started moving now too. My comrades walked past Jiying, but no one said anything. Just as we were swinging around the wall of the school, I turned around and looked at him one last time. He was crouched down in the middle of the flowers. I couldn't see his face clearly. His bent over body among the butterfly flowers waving in the wind, gave me the feeling of flying.

After that I found a bottle of milk in my drawer six times. And as if by a miracle I started to feel a twinge in my chest. A vague sense of pride kept me from feeling sad anymore, even though I wasn't on the list of candidates for the Little Red Guard. And I liked to look at Jiying's back, bending forward listening to the teachers.

LITTLE BALL

The first time I met Little Ball was before the Cultural Revolution. Mother was going to talk with Professor Bai, her father, and took me along. They lived in an apartment with a large, well-lit living room. Most of the furniture was made of sandalwood and finished with a deep-red lacquer. On the tall, broad backs of the chairs were carvings of dancing dragons and phoenixes. They felt cool and refreshing when I touched them. I couldn't keep myself from running my hand over these lifelike figures, from dragon to phoenix, from head to tail. And then I turned around. Behind me stood a little girl who was looking at me with a sweet smile on her round face. She was so little, barely reached my shoulders. When she smiled, her two tiny eyes were as round as two black beans. Her name was Little Ball. I was about to turn six and she was almost nine.

Little Ball motioned me into her room. The room was

small, but neat and orderly. We sat down on the bed, but she didn't say anything. I looked at her and could understand from the expression on her face that she was friendly and happy. I discovered that her eyelashes were long and dark. They hung down, almost covering the two black beans. If you didn't know better, you'd think she was sleeping. I suggested that we go outdoors and play. She shook her head. Mother and I were there for over an hour and she never said a word. But I could see that she liked me.

Two years went by like the wind. My mother and Little Ball's father were both sent away to work in the countryside. I don't remember exactly why my girlfriends and I chose Little Ball's home as a place to gather and play *guai*. It could have been because Little Ball's mother was so friendly and didn't mind all the noise we kids made. While we played, Little Ball sat on the edge of her bed and watched. When the game was at its height, she smiled, but she never showed her teeth or uttered a sound. Little Ball walked to and from school, but she never went out and played with the other kids. In the two years that had gone by, I'd grown a head taller. But Little Ball was just as little as before.

"Little Ball, come play with us!" I said taking her hand to show her how it was done. "Look, it's really simple." I threw the ping-pong ball up in the air, lay the four knucklebones down, and caught the ball before it hit the ground. "Come on, now you try," everyone said together. Little Ball couldn't resist our appeal. She tried a couple times with no luck, and then a few more times. She was actually doing better. And then, surprisingly, Little Ball pulled away and threw herself on the bed. She stared down at the floor. "I can't do it!"

The rest of us played on. Our hands got dirty, and beads

of perspiration gathered on our foreheads and the tips of our noses. It was late. We threw on our winter jackets and left in a hurry. The next day I remembered that I'd forgotten my *guai* game at Little Ball's. I hurried over to Little Ball's home. The door was opened, but Little Ball had no intention of letting me in. I asked if she'd seen my *guai* game. Little Ball was standing with her face right in the crack of the door, and she blushed. She was clearly nervous and stammered, "No, no, it, it is . . . isn't here." I felt it was a little embarrassing and didn't ask again. Confused, I went back home.

The pieces in my *guai* game were the very finest sheep's knuckles. But even though I was very fond of them, they were soon forgotten. There were so many exciting outdoor games and I was interested in so many other things.

Not long afterwards I heard that Little Ball had quit school. It was said that it was due to illness and that she stayed at home all the time. There was so much happening at school—wall posters almost everywhere in every imaginable color, revolutionary songs streaming through the loudspeakers nonstop. Students, teachers and parents worked round the clock building a bomb shelter on the sports field. Everyone had to work, women and men, young and old. I spent the entire day at the building site helping to transport clay and bricks. Such a lot of fun. Nothing could be worse than being sick now, I thought.

Aunt Yang, one of the leaders of the neighborhood committee, expended all her energy mobilizing people to participate in the building project. She shouted, her voice charged with emotion, "Come on, everyone! We're not going to leave anything but an empty city to the ugly bear's jet bombers!" One day even Little Ball was drawn out by the passionate appeal. I hadn't seen her for at least half a year. She was still just as short as before. She slowly approached the building site and the throng of busy people. Her steps appeared to be light, but it wasn't difficult to see that the decision to come outdoors had not been an easy one. The bright sunlight fell heavily on the thin little body, the blue threadbare Mao-jacket, the pale and bashful face. Little Ball lifted a pickax that weighed at least ten pounds and immediately fainted. "Oh, poor girl," people sighed sympathetically. Little Ball was carried away.

"Aunt Yang really gets results. Even a little dwarf was tempted to come out and work."

"Why doesn't she grow?"

"How do you think people can grow when they stay indoors all day long?"

People burst out laughing and talk about Little Ball came to an end. A grown lady took the pickax that had toppled Little Ball and swung it up in the air. . . .

I thought about Little Ball. That same evening I left the building site early and went to her home. Little Ball's mother opened the door and smiled sweetly, as always. From the partially opened door to Little Ball's room I could hear that someone was playing *guai*. It was a familiar and beautiful sound that only my pieces could make, and that I hadn't heard for a long time. I only exchanged a couple words with Little Ball's mother before rushing past her into Little Ball's room. I opened the door and saw Little Ball sitting stiffly on the bed. There was no sign on the floor of any *guai* game. "Little Ball, how are you feeling now?" She nodded imperceptibly and stared nervously at her feet. I stood next to her.

A long silence followed. I broke it. "Why don't you go to school any more?"

"I'm sick," she answered softly.

"What kind of sickness?" Tears came to her eyes. I didn't dare ask any more.

Instead I suggested that we play *guai* together. Little Ball looked at me out of the corner of her eye, but didn't say a word. She thought it over a couple seconds and then gave a nod, as if she'd made an important decision. She turned and pulled out a little packet from under the pillow. It was a flowered handkerchief. She opened the handkerchief and shoved it and the contents toward me. She blushed. "They're really yours, and now you can have them back." Her voice was so low it reminded me of a mosquito's drone. There they were, five knuckles and a ping-pong ball, all as white as snow. I could see they'd been washed many times. "Now they're yours," I said and shoved the packet back to her. She looked at me, happy and relieved.

We played together for a long time, until the people on the building site had packed up for the day. I felt exhausted and carelessly threw myself down on the bed. Little Ball said it was dirty on the floor and insisted that I wash my hands. She stood next to me and carefully washed the *guai* pieces, one by one, while I washed my hands. I looked at her and thought the name Little Ball fit her very well— her round face, her rounded nose, round eyes and round features. I thought it and didn't notice that I also said it. Little Ball was embarrassed and nudged me with her elbow. And then she quietly asked, "Can you tell me why I don't grow?"

"Don't worry about it. People say that some grow early

and others much later. I'm one of those who grows early."
This was something I'd heard from Grandmother.

"You see, many people call me a dwarf. I . . . I'm . . .
afraid."

"Horse? Oh!" I hadn't understood what she said right
away, and added, "Horses are big and strong. When they
call you that, it must mean something good. It's nothing to
be afraid of."

She nudged me with her elbow again. "Now you're jok-
ing. They don't say 'horse,' they say 'dwarf.'"

I didn't understand the word, nor why she was making
such a fuss. But it appeared that Little Ball was still worried.
I jumped off the bed where we'd been sitting and took a red
pencil from my school bag. I stood right up against the wall
and drew a line above my head. "Just jump up to the line,
again and again, and in a few days you'll be that tall."

Little Ball believed that. She measured exactly the difference between herself and the line, and started to jump. She
used all her strength in every single jump, and after only six
or seven jumps she was out of breath and her face was pale.
I quickly helped her to the bed. "I'll take a little break and
then I'll continue," Little Ball said apologetically, her eyes
on the red line. Then she turned her gaze toward me and
smiled. That was the only time I clearly saw her white teeth.
It was late in the evening. Little Ball came out into the hallway with me and asked expectantly, "You're coming again
tomorrow, aren't you? Aren't you? You will, won't you?"

The next day I ate dinner early and went over to Little
Ball's as planned. I knocked on the door, but no one answered. I thought that was a little strange, so I walked around
the building and up to the window to Little Ball's room.

There was no light at all in there. The darkened window on the wall of the large building looked like Little Ball's black eyes, filled with fear. And the half-lowered curtain brought to mind Little Ball's long eyelashes.

A couple days later I heard that Little Ball had disappeared.

Finally one day the door to Little Ball's home was opened. Her mother took hold of me and clutched me tightly. Then she burst into tears, shook me and sobbed, "Tell me, tell me. Where has she gone?" Sobbing, she shook me for a long time. My bones felt like they were coming loose. She stopped suddenly and stared at me, as if she'd understood I was a little girl and not a piece of wood. She started massaging my wobbly neck while she cried. I went into Little Ball's room and peeked around. I slipped my hand under the pillow and felt around. I understood that the *guai* game was no longer there. "Are you looking for something?" Her mother leaned against the doorjamb and asked hesitantly. I didn't answer.

I lived with uncertainty for many years. I was already in high school when one day Little Ball's father appeared. He'd come to discuss some professional matter with Mother. I gathered my courage and asked about Little Ball. "Oh," he sighed deeply. "God knows what's happened to Little Ball. The last afternoon she was home, we received a letter from the school. It said that no one would be exempted from the revolutionary work at school without an excuse, and those who were sick had to be examined and present a doctor's certificate. Little Ball went out before dinner, and hasn't been seen since. But I've always had the feeling that one day she'll come bouncing back. I've believed that all along," the old professor mumbled.

Little Ball never came back.

Twenty years later. I wandered around alone in the dark evening. I peered in through the window to Little Ball's room and understood that a new family had moved in. My thoughts gave my nearsighted eyes extra power, and I could actually see the red line on the wall very clearly. A height Little Ball pushed herself to the limit to reach.

"Little Ball, where have you been hiding all these years, playing *guai?*" I whispered.

GLOSSARY

phoenix   A large and beautiful bird in Chinese mythology.

gou-zai-zi   "Puppies"; name often used for children of counterrevolutionaries.

guai   An animal knuckle used in a popular girls' game.

gui   "Back," "return" or "come back home."

heibang   "Black gang"; popular term for so-called reactionary forces during the Cultural Revolution.

jiao-lian   Traditional practice of removing hair from a woman's head when she marries, to make her forehead appear larger. This is done by winding a thread around the hair and then pulling the hair out by the thread.

Jinggang Shan   Mountain range in Southern China where Mao Zedong led his first campaign for Communism in the 1920s.

nanmu   A type of wood that is very hard and dense, often used to build fine furniture.

suona   A Chinese brass instrument similar to a trumpet.

ABOUT THE AUTHOR

Today He Dong lives and works in Oslo, Norway, but she lived the first twenty-five years of her life in Beijing, the city where all but one of the stories in this collection are set. He Dong studied at China University of Physical Education, earning a degree in sport physiology in 1982. In 1985 she was accepted for post-graduate study in biology at the University of Trondheim, and since that time has made Norway her home. She currently holds a research position at the University of Oslo and also runs her own acupuncture clinic.

In the midst of this busy work schedule, He Dong pursues her writing career as author and translator. She has published books both in China and in Norway. Chinese publications include a collection of her poems, *Thin Moon,* 1990; translations of poems by contemporary Norwegian poets, *Polaris,* 1992; a translation of the poetry of Henrik Ibsen in 1995. A second volume of He Dong's poems, *Himmel Innsjø* (*Heaven Lake*) was published in Norway, in both Chinese and Norwegian translation, in 1994. The present collection of short stories, titled *Spør solen,* appeared in 1995.

ABOUT THE TRANSLATOR

Katherine Hanson was the editor and translator of many of the selections in *An Everyday Story: Norwegian Women's Fiction,* first published by Seal Press in 1984. Ten years later she compiled an expanded edition of this anthology which includes a story by He Dong (Women in Translation, 1995). In collaboration with Judith Messick, Hanson has translated three novels by the nineteenth-century Norwegian author Amalie Skram: *Constance Ring, Professor Hieronimus* and *St. Jørgen's* (the latter two books were published under one title, *Under Observation*).

TRANSLATOR'S NOTE

Translating is a collaborative process. The translator's most important partner is, of course, the author, whose presence in the text serves both to inspire and discipline. When the author is living, there is the possibility of a more tangible collaboration, and I have been most fortunate to have been able to carry on an electronic dialogue with He Dong while translating the six stories in this volume. In the case of He Dong's stories the problems I faced as a translator were compounded by the fact that I was working from a Norwegian translation of texts originally written in Chinese. He Dong wrote these stories while living in Norway, and they were first published by a Norwegian publishing house; to date this collection of stories has not been published in the original language, Chinese. But just as He Dong worked with her Norwegian translators, she has answered my countless queries with detailed explanations and commentary, and has even provided illustrations where words failed! Needless to say, I am indebted to the care and thoroughness with which she has helped me recast her texts into yet another foreign language.

And there are others who have helped me along the way. Without the financial support of the National Endowment of the Arts and NORLA (Norwegian Literature Abroad) this book would not have been possible—a thousand thanks to both institutions. I would also like to thank Clare Conrad and Rebecca Engrav for the care and creativity they brought to cover and text design. Jane Hanson found words and phrasing that had been eluding me for weeks, and I thank her. I am, as always, deeply appreciative of Barbara Wilson's keen ear and critical eye and her patience and insight in helping me find solutions to sticky problems. Finally, my thanks go out to Michael Schick for spending so much time on these stories with me!

WELCOME TO THE WORLD OF
INTERNATIONAL WOMEN'S WRITING

Wayfarer: New Fiction by Korean Women, edited and translated by Bruce and Ju-Chan Fulton. $14.95. ISBN: 1-879679-09-4. A fresh and powerful collection of short stories by eight of Korea's top women writers. Edited by the award-winning translators of *Words of Farewell.*

The Cockatoo's Lie by Marion Bloem. $11.95. ISBN: 1-879679-08-6. Family history and a steamy love triangle weave together in this modern novel of Dutch-Indonesian cultural identity.

The Four Winds by Gerd Brantenberg. $12.95. ISBN: 1-879679-05-1. Gerd Brantenberg is one of Norway's cultural treasures, and a lesbian author with a huge international following. This is her hilarious and moving novel of coming out in the sixties at the University of Oslo.

Unnatural Mothers by Renate Dorrestein. $11.95. ISBN: 1-879679-06-X. One of the most original novels to appear from Holland in years, this compelling story of an archeologist and his eleven-year-old daughter's attempts to build a family is by turns satiric and heartbreaking.

An Everyday Story: Norwegian Women's Fiction edited by Katherine Hanson. $14.95. ISBN: 1-879679-07-8. Norway's tradition of storytelling comes alive in this enthralling anthology. The new expanded edition includes stories by contemporary writers.

Unmapped Territories: New Women's Fiction from Japan edited by Yukiko Tanaka. $10.95. ISBN: 1-879679-00-0. These stunning new stories by well-known and emerging writers chart a world of vanishing social and physical landmarks in a Japan both strange and familiar. With an insightful introduction by Tanaka on the literature and culture of the "era of women" in Japan.

Two Women in One by Nawal el-Saadawi. $9.95. ISBN: 1-879679-01-9. One of this Egyptian feminist's most important novels, *Two Women in One* tells the story of Bahiah Shaheen, a well-behaved Cairo medical student—and her other side: rebellious, political and artistic.

Under Observation by Amalie Skram. With an introduction by Elaine Showalter. $15.95. ISBN: 1-879679-03-5. This riveting story of a woman painter confined against her will in a Copenhagen asylum is a classic of nineteenth century Norwegian literature by the author of *Constance Ring* and *Betrayed*.

How Many Miles to Babylon by Doris Gercke. $8.95. ISBN: 1-879679-02-7. Hamburg police detective Bella Block needs a vacation. She thinks she'll find some rest in the countryside, but after only a few hours in the remote village of Roosbach, she realizes she has stumbled onto one of the most troubling cases of her career. The first of this provocative German author's thrillers to be translated into English.

Wild Card by Assumpta Margenat. $8.95. ISBN: 1-879679-04-3. Translated from the Catalan, this lively mystery is set in Andorra, a tiny country in the Pyrenees. Rocio is a supermarket clerk bored with her job and her sexist boss. One day she devises a scheme to get ahead in the world. . . .

Women in Translation is a nonprofit publishing company, dedicated to making women's fiction from around the world available in English translation. The books above may be ordered from us at 523 N. 84th St, Seattle, WA 98103. (Please include $3.00 postage and handling for the first book and 50¢ for each additional book.) Write to us for a free catalog.